Antarctica

by the same author

WALK THE BLUE FIELDS
FOSTER
SMALL THINGS LIKE THESE
SO LATE IN THE DAY

CLAIRE KEEGAN

Antarctica

faber

First published in 1999
by Faber & Faber Ltd
The Bindery, 51 Hatton Garden
London EC1N 8HN

This paperback edition first published in 2023

Typeset by Faber & Faber Ltd
Printed and bound by CPI Group (UK) Ltd, Croydon CR0 4YY

'The Ginger Rogers Sermon' was first published
in *Phoenix Irish Short Stories* in August 1997.
'The Singing Cashier' first appeared in the *Paris Review*,
Spring 1998, and was broadcast on RTE.
'Storms' and 'Quare Name for a Boy' were also broadcast on RTE.
'Burns' was first published in *Force 10* and broadcast on RTE.
'Where the Water's Deepest' was published in the *Sunday Tribune*
and broadcast on RTE in 1996.
'Passport Soup' was first published in the *Mail on Sunday*
and was broadcast by the BBC World Service.

A CIP record for this book is available from the British Library

ISBN 978-0-571-38221-7

Printed and bound in the UK on FSC® certified paper in line with our continuing
commitment to ethical business practices, sustainability and the environment.

For further information see faber.co.uk/environmental-policy

2 4 6 8 10 9 7 5 3 1

For Padraig Hickey, who rescued me in a time of floods
and in memory of John McCarron, teacher.

Contents

Acknowledgements, viii

Antarctica, 3
Love in the Tall Grass, 23
Where the Water's Deepest, 39
The Ginger Rogers Sermon, 47
Storms, 69
The Singing Cashier, 77
Burns, 85
Quare Name for a Boy, 95
Ride if You Dare, 103
Men and Women, 119
Sisters, 137
A Scent of Winter, 163
You Can't Be Too Careful, 171
The Burning Palms, 189
Passport Soup, 201

Acknowledgements

Much thanks to David Marcus, Giles Gordon, Mary McCay, the Tyrone Guthrie Centre at Annaghmakerrig, and friends and faculty at the University of Wales, Cardiff, and Trinity College, Dublin.

Antarctica

Antarctica

Every time the happily married woman went away she wondered how it would feel to sleep with another man. That weekend she was determined to find out. It was December; she felt a curtain closing on another year. She wanted to do this before she got too old. She was sure she would be disappointed.

On Friday evening, she took the train into the city, sat reading in a first-class carriage. The crime novel didn't hold her interest; she could already predict the ending. She stared out beyond the window. A few lighted houses, fiery points, flashed past her in the darkness. She had left a dish of macaroni cheese out for the kids, brought her husband's suits back from the cleaners. She'd told him she was going shopping for Christmas. He'd no reason not to trust her.

When she reached the city she took a taxi to the hotel. They gave her a small, white room with a view of Vicar's Close, one of the oldest streets in England, a row of stone houses with tall, granite chimneys where the clergy lived. She sat at the hotel bar that night nursing a tequila and lime, but there was nothing doing. Old men were reading newspapers, business was slow, but she didn't mind; she needed a good night's sleep. She fell into her rented bed, into a dreamless sleep, and woke to the sound of bells ringing in the cathedral.

On Saturday she walked to the shopping centre. Families were out, pushing buggies through the morning crowd, a thick stream of people flowing through glass automatic doors. She bought unusual gifts for her children, things she thought they wouldn't predict. She bought an electric razor for her eldest son – he was getting to that age – an atlas for the girl, and for her husband an expensive gold watch with a plain, white face.

She dressed up in the afternoon, put on a short plum-coloured dress, high heels, her darkest lipstick, and walked back into town. A jukebox song, 'The Ballad of Lucy Jordan', lured her into a pub, a converted prison with barred windows and a low, beamed ceiling. Fruit machines blinked in one corner and just as she sat on a bar stool a little battalion of coins fell into a shoot. On the next stool sat a guy in a leather jacket that looked like he should have given it to Oxfam years ago.

'Hello,' he said. 'Haven't seen you before.' He had a red complexion, a gold chain dangling inside a Hawaiian print shirt, mud-coloured hair. His glass was almost empty.

'What's that you're drinking?' she said.

He turned out to be a real talker, told her his life story, how he worked nights at the old folks' home. How he lived alone, was an orphan, had no relations except a distant cousin he'd never met. There were no rings on his fingers.

'I'm the loneliest man in the world,' he said. 'How about you?'

'I'm married.' She said it before she knew what she was saying.

He laughed. 'Play pool with me.'

'I don't know how.'

'Doesn't matter,' he said, 'I'll teach you. You'll be potting that black before you know it.' He put coins into a slot and pulled something and a little landslide of balls knuckled down into a black hole under the table.

'Stripes and solids,' he said, chalking up the cue. 'You're one or the other. I'll break.'

He taught her to lean down low and sight the ball, to watch the cue ball when she took the shot, but he didn't let her win one game. When she went into the ladies' room, she was drunk. She couldn't find the end of the toilet paper. She leaned her forehead against the cool of the mirror. She couldn't remember ever being drunk like this. They finished off their drinks and went outside. The air spiked her lungs. Clouds smashed into each other in the sky. She hung her head back to look at them. She wished the world could turn into a fabulous, outrageous red to match her mood.

'Let's walk,' he said. 'I'll give you the tour.'

She fell into step beside him, listened to his jacket creaking as he led her down a path where the moat curved round the cathedral. An old man stood outside the Bishop's Palace selling stale bread for the birds. They bought some and stood at the water's edge feeding five cygnets whose feathers were turning white. Brown ducks flew across the water and landed in a nice skim on the moat. When a black Labrador came bounding down the path, a huddle of pigeons rose as one and settled magically in the trees.

'I feel like Francis of Assisi,' she laughed.

Rain began to fall; she felt it falling on her face like small electric shocks. They backtracked through the market-place where stalls were set up in the shelter of tarpaulin. They sold everything: smelly second-hand books and china dishes, big red poinsettias, holly wreaths, brass ornaments, fresh fish with dead eyes lying on a bed of ice.

'Come home with me,' he said. 'I'll cook for you.'

'You'll cook for me?'

'You eat fish?'

'I eat everything,' she said, and he seemed amused.

'I know your type,' he said. 'You're wild. You're one of those wild middle-class women.'

He chose a trout that looked like it was still alive. The fishmonger chopped its head off and wrapped it up in foil. He bought a tub of black olives and a slab of feta cheese from the Italian woman with the deli stall at the end. He bought limes and Colombian coffee. Always, as they passed the stalls, he asked her if she wanted anything. He was free with his money, kept it crumpled in his pockets like old receipts, didn't smooth the notes out even when he was handing them over. On the way home they stopped at the off-licence, bought two bottles of Chianti and a lottery ticket, all of which she insisted on paying for.

'We'll split it if we win,' she said. 'Go to the Bahamas.'

'Don't hold your breath,' he said, and watched her walk through the door he'd opened for her. They strolled down cobbled streets, past a barber's where a man was sitting with his head back, being shaved. The streets grew narrow and winding; they were outside the city lights now.

'You live in suburbia?' she asked.

He did not answer, kept walking. She could smell the fish. When they came to a wrought-iron gate he told her to 'hang a left'. They passed under an archway and came out in a dead end. He unlocked a door to a block of flats and followed her upstairs to the top floor.

'Keep going,' he said when she stopped on the landings. She giggled and climbed, giggled and climbed again, stopped at the top.

The door needed oil; the hinges creaked when he pushed it back. The walls of his flat were plain and pale, the sills dusty. One stained mug sat lonely in the sink. A white Persian cat jumped off a draylon couch in the living room. It was neglected, like a place where someone used to live; the rubber plant in the lounge crawled across the carpet towards a rectangular pool of streetlight under a high window. Dank smells. No sign of a phone, no photographs, no decorations, no Christmas tree.

A big cast-iron tub stood in the bathroom on blue, steel claws.

'Some bath,' she said.

'You want a bath?' he said. 'Try it out. Fill her up and dive in. Go ahead, be my guest.'

She filled the tub, kept the water as hot as she could stand it. He came in and stripped to the waist, and shaved at the handbasin with his back to her. She closed her eyes and listened to him work the lather, tapping the razor against the sink, shaving. It was like they'd done it all before. She thought him the least threatening man she'd ever known. She held her nose and slid under-water, listened to the blood pumping in her head, the rush and cloud in her brain. When she surfaced, he was standing there in the steam, wiping traces of shaving foam off his chin, smiling.

'Having fun?' he said.

When he lathered a flannel, she got up. Water fell off her shoulders and trickled down her legs. He began at her feet and worked upwards, washing her in strong, slow circles. She looked good in the yellow shaving light, raised her feet and arms and turned like a child for him. He made her sink back down into the water and rinsed her off, wrapped her in a towel.

'I know what you need,' he said. 'You need looking after. There isn't a woman on the earth who doesn't need looking after. Stay there.' He went out and came back with a comb, began combing the knots from her hair. 'Look at you,' he said. 'You're a real blonde. You've blonde fuzz, like a peach.' His knuckle slid down the back of her neck, followed her vertebrae.

[8]

His bed was brass with a white, goose-down duvet and black pillowcases. She undid his belt, slid it from the loops. The buckle jingled when it hit the floor. She loosened his trousers. Naked, he wasn't beautiful, yet there was something voluptuous about him, something unbreakable and sturdy in his build. His skin was hot.

'Pretend you're America,' she said. 'I'll be Columbus.'

Under the bedclothes, down between the damp of his thighs, she explored his nakedness. His body was a novelty. When her feet became entangled in the sheets, he flung them off. She had surprising strength in bed, an urgency that bruised him. She pulled his head back by the hair, drank in the smell of strange soap on his neck. He kissed her and kissed her. There wasn't any hurry. His palms were the rough hands of a working man. They battled against their lust, wrestled against what in the end carried them away. Afterwards they smoked – she hadn't smoked in years, quit before the first baby. She was reaching over for the ashtray when she saw the shotgun cartridge behind his clock-radio.

'What's this?' She picked it up. It was heavier than it looked.

'Oh that. That's a present for somebody.'

'Some present,' she said. 'Looks like pool isn't the only thing you shoot.' She said this and laughed.

'Come here.'

She snuggled up against him, and they fell swiftly into sleep, the sweet sleep of children, and woke in darkness, hungry.

[9]

While he took charge of dinner, she sat in the couch with the cat on her lap and watched a documentary on Antarctica, miles of snow, penguins shuffling against the sub-zero winds, Captain Cook sailing down to find the lost continent, icebergs. He came out with a tea towel draped across his shoulder and handed her a glass of chilled Chianti.

'You,' he said, 'have a thing for explorers.' He leaned down over the back of the couch and kissed her.

'Can I do anything?' she asked.

'No,' he said and went back into the kitchen.

She sipped her wine and felt her throat opening again, cold sliding down into her stomach. She could hear him chopping vegetables, the bubble of water boiling on the stove. Dinner smells drifted through the rooms. Coriander, lime juice, onions. She could stay drunk; she could live like this. He came out and laid two places at table, lit a thick, green candle, folded paper napkins. They looked like small white pyramids under a vigil of flame. She turned the TV off, and stroked the cat. Its white hairs fell on to his dark-blue dressing gown that was much too big for her. She saw the smoke from another man's fire cross the window, but she did not think about her husband, and her lover never mentioned her home life either, not once.

Instead, over Greek salad and grilled trout the conversation somehow turned to the subject of Hell.

As a child, she had been told that Hell was different for everyone, your own worst possible scenario. 'I always thought Hell would be unbearably cold, a place where you stayed half-frozen but you never quite lost consciousness and you never really felt anything,' she said. 'There'd be nothing, only a cold sun and the Devil there, watching you.' She shivered and shook herself. Her colour was high. She put her glass to her lips and tilted her neck back as she swallowed. She had a nice, long neck.

'In that case,' he said, 'Hell for me would be deserted; there'd be nobody there. Not even the Devil. I've always taken heart in the fact that Hell is populated; all my friends will be there.' He ground more pepper over his salad plate and tore the doughy heart out of the loaf.

'The nun at school told us it would last for all eternity,' she said, pulling the skin off her trout. 'And when we asked how long eternity lasted, she said: "Think of all the sand in the world, all the beaches, all the sand quarries, the ocean beds, the deserts. Now imagine all that sand in an hour-glass, like a gigantic egg-timer. If one grain of sand drops every year, eternity is the length of time it takes for all the sand in the world to pass through that glass." Just think! That terrified us. We were very young.'

'You don't still believe in Hell?' he said.

'No. Can't you tell? If only Sister Emmanuel could see me now, fucking a complete stranger, what a laugh.' She broke off a flake of trout and ate it with her fingers.

He put his cutlery down, folded his hands in his lap and looked at her. She was full now, playing with her food.

'So you think all your friends will be in Hell too,' she said. 'That's nice.'

'Not by your nun's definition.'

'You have lots of friends? I suppose you know people from work.'

'A few,' he said. 'And you?'

'I have two good friends,' she said. 'Two people I'd die for.'

'You're lucky,' he said, and got up to make the coffee.

That night, he was ravenous, like a man leasing himself out to her. There was nothing he wouldn't do.

'You're a very generous lover,' she said afterwards, passing him the cigarette. 'You're very generous full stop.'

The cat jumped up on the bed and startled her.

'Jesus Christ!' she said. There was something creepy about his cat.

Cigarette ash fell on the duvet but they were too drunk to care. Drunk and careless and occupying the same bed on the same night. It was all so simple, really. Loud Christmas music started up in the apartment downstairs. A Gregorian chant, monks singing.

'Who's your neighbour?'

'Oh, some granny. Deaf as a coot. She sings too. She's on her own down there; keeps odd hours.'

They settled down to sleep, she with her head captured in the crook of his shoulder. He stroked her arm, petting her like an animal. She imitated the cat purring, rolling her 'r's the way they'd taught her in Spanish class while hailstones rapped the window panes.

'I'll miss you when you go,' he whispered.

She said nothing, just lay there watching the red numbers on his clock-radio change until she drifted off.

On Sunday she woke early. A white frost had fallen in the night. She dressed, watched him sleeping, his head on the black pillow. In the bathroom she looked inside the cabinet. It was empty. In the lounge, she read the titles of his books. They were arranged in alphabetical order. She walked back along treacherous pavements to check out of her hotel. She got lost and had to ask a troubled-looking lady with a poodle where to go. A huge Christmas tree sparkled in the lobby. Her suitcase lay open on the bed. Her clothes smelled of cigarette smoke. She showered and changed. The cleaning lady knocked at ten but she waved her off, told her not to bother, told her nobody should work on Sundays.

In the lobby, she sat in the telephone booth and called home. She asked about the children, the weather, asked her husband about his day, told him about the children's gifts. She would return to untidy, cluttered rooms, dirty floors, cut knees, a hall with mountain-bikes and roller-skates. Questions. She hung up, became aware of a presence behind her, waiting.

'You never said goodbye.' She felt his breath on her neck.

He was standing there, a black wool cap pulled down low over his ears, hiding his forehead.

'You were sleeping,' she said.

'You sneaked off,' he said. 'You're a sneaky one.'

'I –'

'You want to sneak off to lunch and get drunk?' He pushed her into the booth and kissed her, a long, wet kiss. 'I woke this morning with your scent in the sheets,' he said. 'It was beautiful.'

'Bottle it,' she said, 'we'll make a fortune.'

They ate lunch in a place with six-foot walls, arched windows and a flagstone floor. Their table was next to a fire. Over plates of roast beef and Yorkshire pudding they got drunk again, but they didn't talk much. She drank Bloody Marys, told the waitress to go heavy on the Tabasco. He started on ale then switched to gin and tonics, anything to stave off the imminent prospect of their separation.

'I don't normally drink like this,' she said. 'How about you?'

'Nah,' he said, and signalled the waitress for another round.

They dawdled over dessert and the Sunday newspapers. The landlady came round and threw more wood on the fire. Once, while turning a page of the newspaper, she looked up. He was staring intently at her mouth.

'Smile,' he said.

'What?'

'Smile.'

She smiled and he reached over and pressed the tip of his index finger against her tooth.

'There,' he said, showing her a tiny speck of food. 'It's gone now.'

When they walked out on to the market-place, a thick fog had fallen on the town, so thick she could hardly read the signs. A straggle of Sunday vendors, out to win the Christmas trade, were demonstrating their wares.

'Done your Christmas shopping?' she said.

'Nah, got nobody to buy for, have I? I'm an orphan. Remember?'

'I'm sorry.'

'Come on. Let's walk.'

He gripped her hand and took her down a dirt road that led into a black wood beyond the houses.

'You're hurting me,' she said.

He loosened his hold but he did not say sorry. Light drained out of that day. Dusk stoked the sky, bribing daylight into darkness. They walked for a long time without talking, just feeling the Sunday hush, listening to the trees straining against the icy wind.

'I was married once, went off to Africa for a honeymoon,' he said suddenly. 'It didn't last. I had a big house, furniture, all that. She was a good woman too, a wonderful gardener. You know that plant in my lounge? Well, that was hers. I've been waiting for years for that plant to die, but the fucking thing, it keeps on growing.'

She pictured the plant sprawled across the floor, the length of a grown man, its pot no bigger than a small saucepan, dried roots snarling up over the pot. A miracle it was still alive.

'Some things you just have no control over,' he said, scratching his head. 'She said I wouldn't last a year without her. Boy, was she wrong.' He looked at her then, and smiled, a strange smile of victory.

They had walked deep into the woods by now; except for the sound of their footsteps on the road and the ribbon of sky between the trees, she could not have been sure where the path was. He grabbed her suddenly and pulled her in under the trees, pushed her back against a tree-trunk. She couldn't see. She felt the bark through her coat, his belly against hers, could smell gin on his breath.

'You won't forget me,' he said, smoothing her hair back from her eyes. 'Say it. Say you won't forget me.'

'I won't forget you,' she said.

In the darkness, he ran his fingers across her face, same as he was a blind man trying to memorise her. 'Nor I, you. A little piece of you will be ticking right here,' he said, taking her hand and placing it inside his shirt. She felt his heart beneath his hot skin, beating. He kissed her then as if there was something in her mouth he wanted. Words, probably. At that moment the cathedral bells rang and she wondered what time it was. Her train left at six but she was all packed, there was no real hurry.

'Did you check out this morning?'

'Yes,' she laughed. 'They think I'm the tidiest guest they've ever had. My bag's in the lobby.'

'Come to my place. I'll get you a taxi, see you off.'

She wasn't in the mood for sex. In her mind she had already packed up and left, was facing her husband in

[16]

the doorway. She felt clean and full and warm; all she wanted now was a good snooze on the train. But in the end she could think of no reason not to go and, yielding like a parting gift to him, said yes.

They retreated from the darkness of the woods, walked down Vicar's Close and emerged below the moat near the hotel. The seagulls were inland. They hovered above the water fowl, swooping down and snapping up the bread a bunch of Americans were throwing to the swans. She collected her suitcase and walked the slippery streets to his place. The rooms were cold. Yesterday's dirty dishes lay soaking in the sink, a rim of greasy water on the steel. Remnant daylight filtered through gaps between the curtains, but he did not turn a light on.

'Come here,' he said. He took his jacket off and knelt before her. He unlaced her boots, undid the knots slowly, peeled her stockings off, eased her underwear down around her ankles. He stood up and took her coat off, opened her blouse carefully, admired the buttons, unzipped her skirt, slid her watch down over her hand. Then he reached up under her hair and took her earrings out. They were dangly earrings, gold leaves her husband had given her for their anniversary. He stripped her as if he had all the time in the world. She felt like a child being put to bed. She didn't have to do anything to him, for him. No duties, all she had to do was be there.

'Lie back,' he said.

Naked, she fell back into the goose-down.

'I could go to sleep,' she said, shutting her eyes.

'Not yet,' he said.

The room was cold, but he was sweating; she could smell his sweat. He pinned her wrists back above her head with one hand and kissed her throat. A drop of sweat fell on to her neck. A drawer opened and something jingled. Handcuffs. She was startled, but did not think fast enough to object.

'You'll like this,' he said. 'Trust me.'

He bound her wrists to the brass bed-head. A section of her mind panicked. There was something deliberate about him, something silent and overpowering. More sweat fell on her. She tasted the tangy salt on his skin. He retreated and advanced, made her ask for it, made her come.

He got up. He went out and left her there, handcuffed to the headboard. The kitchen light came on. She smelled coffee, heard him breaking eggs. He came in with a tray and sat over her.

'I have to –'

'Don't move.' He said it very quietly. He was dead calm.

'Take these off –'

'Shhhhh,' he said. 'Eat. Eat before you go.' He extended a bite of scrambled egg on a fork and she swallowed it. It tasted of salt and pepper. She turned her head. The clock read 5:32.

'Christ, look at the time –'

'Don't swear,' he said. 'Eat. And drink. Drink this. I'll get the keys.'

'Why won't you –'

'Just take a drink. Come on. I drank with you, remember?'

Still handcuffed, she drank the coffee he tilted from the mug. It only took a minute. A warm, dark feeling spread over her and then she slept.

When she woke, he was standing in the harsh fluorescent light, dressing. She was still handcuffed to the bed. She tried to speak. She was gagged. One of her ankles, too, was bound to the foot of the bed with another pair of handcuffs. He continued dressing, clipping the studs of his denim shirt closed.

'I have to go to work,' he said, tying his bootlaces. 'It can't be helped.'

He went out, came back in with a basin. 'In case you need it,' he said, leaving it on the bed. He tucked her in and kissed her then, a quick, normal kiss, and turned the light out. He stopped in the hall and turned to face her. His shadow loomed over the bed. Her eyes were very big and pleading. She was reaching out to him with her eyes. He held his hands out, showing his palms.

'It's not what you think,' he said. 'It really isn't. I love you, you see. Try to understand.'

And then he turned and left. She listened to him leave, heard him on the stairs, a zipper closing. The hall light was doused, the door banged, she heard his walk on the pavement, footsteps ebbing.

Frantic, she tried her best to undo the handcuffs. She did everything to get free. She was a strong woman. She tried to disconnect the headboard, but when she nudged the sheet back, she could see the bed-head, bolted to the frame. For a long time she rattled the bed. She wanted to yell 'fire!' – that's what police told women to yell in emergencies – but she couldn't chew through the cloth. She managed to get her loose foot on the floor and thumped the carpet. Then she remembered granny, deaf, downstairs. Hours passed before she calmed down to think and listen. Her breathing steadied. She heard the curtain flapping in the next room. He'd left the window open. The duvet had fallen on the floor in all the fuss and she was naked. She couldn't reach it. Cold was moving in, spilling into the house, filling up the rooms. She shivered. Cold air falls, she thought. Eventually the shivering stopped. Chronic numbness spread through her; she imagined the blood slowing in her veins, her heart shrinking. The cat sprang up and landed on the bed, prowled the mattress. Her dulled rage changed to terror. That too passed. The curtain in the next room slapped the wall faster now: the wind was rising. She thought of him and felt nothing. She thought about her husband and her children. They might never find her. She might never see them again. It didn't matter. She could see her own breath in the gloom, feel the cold closing over her head. It began to dawn on her, a cold, slow sun bleaching the east. Was it her imagination or was that snow falling beyond the window panes? She watched the clock on his bedside table, the red numbers changing. The cat was watching her, his eyes dark as apple seeds. She thought of Antarctica, the snow and ice and the bodies of dead explorers. Then she thought of Hell, and then eternity.

Love in the Tall Grass

Cordelia wakes on a white-cold afternoon, watches woodsmoke pluming beyond the trembling hedge. She rises, opens the window outward, hears the swoon of matinee music in the road. Winter air teems in on this, the last day of the twentieth century. Cordelia strips naked, pours water from the steel jug, half-fills the basin, wrings out the wash-cloth, soaps her hands, her face. When the pipes burst in late November, she never got the plumber in, broke the ice in the rain-barrel under the shoot and dipped the bucket down. This water is colder than a broken dream. She dries herself and dresses, slowly, in a green dress, fastens the clasp of a platinum locket around her neck. She bends and laces up her flat black shoes, knowing that when this day is over, nothing will ever be the same.

In the kitchen she lowers a little brown egg into an old saucepan, puts the kettle on, takes out the stainless-steel egg-cup, its tarnished spoon, the stripy mug and plate, and waits until it's ready. Somewhere somebody is chopping wood. This kettle always sings before it boils. By the open door she sits. She's slept, now she must eat. She spreads a teacloth across her lap and breaks the shell, salts the egg, spreads butter over bread, pours tea. Withered leaves skid in across the marbled lino. The Burmese believe that wind carrying betel leaves into the bride's house will bring bad luck and unhappiness to the married couple. So many small, useless facts rattle around like old currency inside Cordelia's head. The clock on the mantel ticks happily. Not long now, it seems to say. Not long now. When she's finished, she turns the empty eggshell upside-down, a trick she played in childhood that turned to habit. She takes a handkerchief from her sleeve and wipes her mouth. It is time. She undoes her braid and brushes out her hair. She knows no other woman whose hair's turned white at forty. Lastly, she takes her good black coat from its crook on the back door, opens the latch and goes out into what's left of the December wind.

It is almost nine years since Cordelia has walked this road. It dips down between new bungalows into the village. The Silver Dollar Takeaway stands in darkness; a neglected ice-cream van's wheels sag from the weight of winter neglect, its HB sign well faded, but there's a light in the Lone Star Guesthouse and the little souvenir shop's door is open. She suspects that after the new century's ushered in, they'll clamp closed once again, wait for summer's gaggle of tourists, the trampoline of kids. She becomes aware of faces behind net curtains. She stops at the chapel, slides back the glass porch door, blesses herself with water from the font. Inside, the chapel's empty, the marble altar-railing she remembered, gone. A statue ornaments each side of the altar: the Virgin Mary and Saint Joseph. One in brown, the other blue. Why is Mary always blue? she wonders. She lights a candle at her feet, she looks so lonely. Near the altar stands a coffin covered in cloth, burgundy folds, such a small coffin, but then she realises it's the church organ. She backs down into the empty confession box, slides the grid across and whispers:

'Bless me, Father, for I have sinned.'

That takes her back. A sudden draught travels through the chapel, sounding strangely like a motor race, a high, revving wind. She sits in the bottom pew and opens the missal at random, reads the lesson from Palm Sunday and thinks Judas Iscariot a beautiful name.

Cordelia continues the steep descent. She stops and sits by the roadside, empties a pebble from her shoe. Gorse shelters this road, green, shuddering gorse that bursts into relentless yellow for half the year. It is getting dark; she feels the light draining, watches the blue dusk deepening in the west. She gets up, puts one foot in front of the other. A shroud of mist thickens fast over the barren dunes. She feels her heart beating, feels tired, bone tired, and evening deepens all around her quickly, so very quickly. She still has far to go, two miles or more. She must get there before dark or be lost. She remembers the waiting room, the gleam of the stethoscope on the doctor's table, the promise spoken, the sincerity in his voice, and hurries on.

So too was it dusk when Cordelia met the doctor, a late September dusk of fallen fruit. Exasperated, she had taken a mallet from the shed and driven a staked sign down outside the front gate. APPLES, the sign read. Gale force winds had shaken the trees bare overnight. She'd woken and found the orchard grounds carpeted: Cox's orange pippin, Golden Delicious, Bramley, Red Janets, crab apples. They all lay abundant and bruised in the long grass. She filled buckets, basins, big saucepans, the old Moses basket – but the surplus abounded beneath the trees.

When the doctor's car turned into her driveway, Cordelia was sitting on the steps outside the front door, turning the Jams & Jellies pages of her cook-book. On the window ledge above her head stood jam jars of drowned wasps, their striped bodies floating on the cloudy water. The doctor threw a tall and steady shadow over her. He looked like a man who could jump a fence and climb a tree. She led him up the orchard path, where he took his hands out of his pockets and shook his head.

'Do you have a spade?'

He took his jacket off, rolled up his sleeves. His arms were pale for summer, the pale blue veins in his wrists, his inner arm like a blue branch a child might draw on a white page. But his hands were brown to the wrists, as if he had dipped them in permanent ink that could not be washed off. While the sun burned an orange hole in the sky, the doctor dug a pit in Cordelia's orchard. They lined the pit with straw and carefully laid the apples down so they would not touch.

'There,' he said, 'apples all year round.'

'Come in and wash your hands.'

Her kitchen was dark and cool and smelled strangely of must and something else the doctor could not place. Cordelia gave him the bar of carbolic soap and he washed his hands. She filled a cup with milk, which he drank before he left with a shallow enamel basinful of apples. Cordelia gathered her skirt into a pouch and filled that too. The doctor noticed her knees, marked where she had knelt on the grass, her brown thighs, and thought of them as he drove back home to his wife and children, the fallen apples from Cordelia's orchard rolling around on his back seat.

The doctor came back. He returned the basin, refilled it at Cordelia's insistence, and returned again. It became habitual, on Thursdays, for the doctor to stop, and if the weather was warm, Cordelia and the doctor drank tea outdoors. They leant against the tree-trunks in dappled shade. The doctor dawdled over his tea, sipped it like a girl while the afternoon sun shone bashfully through the trees. Cordelia asked him about medical school, the surgery, and listened. She listened to the words and the accent and the tone, the silences, the hesitation. She noticed he did not mention his wife. Up close, she smelled mothballs in his winter jacket; he smelled like an old drawer that hadn't been opened in a very long time.

On her thirtieth birthday, Cordelia sat with her feet in a basin of hot water all morning and listened to a thunderstorm. She drank three big vodkas with shaken orange juice and tied a ribbon in her hair. When the doctor arrived, she took his hand and led him out under the chestnut tree whose limbs drooped low to the ground. Cordelia used to sit there as a child and imagine she was sitting inside a giant's green skirt. Overhead a patch of blue sky showed through the leaves like a bruised knee.

That afternoon the doctor did not ask for tea. Instead he wound her long yellow hair like a bandage around his hand, and kissed her. It turned dark as night under the tree, so when he looked at the time, he had to put the face of his watch up close to his, then rushed off home, leaving skid-marks in Cordelia's drive.

That night Cordelia lay in bed above the green-dark orchard while drowsy bluebottles struggled against the window panes. She watched the sudden, fast shadows of swallows who flew past her window in fleeting pairs, subtracting light from her room, and marvelled how living things could suspend themselves in mid-air. She lay and listened, imagined she heard the last of the overripe fruit, the latecomers, falling in the slightest breeze. She did not have the heart to pluck them. She heard them falling, imagined the stem weakening, the fruit clinging to its source, losing, loosening, letting go, falling, falling.

The doctor told his wife he was out on house-calls. Because his car was so conspicuous, they started to meet in the sand dunes at Strandhill. They brought drumsticks, flasks of coffee, cake and bars of Belgian chocolate because the doctor had a sweet tooth. On warmer days, he opened his shirt and she kicked her boots off and let her hair down. But mostly they just lay there with Cordelia's big black coat over them, listening to the tide, he with his head hidden in the reeds. Sometimes they fell into shallow sleep, but always Cordelia was aware of the irreversible ticking of the doctor's gold watch: Tick, tick, tick. Not long now, it seemed to say. Not long now. She hated that watch; she wanted to stand up and throw it in the ocean.

Cordelia dreamt of them together in a room with a green, flapping curtain she could not pull back. She could see out, but nobody would ever be able to see in. When she told the doctor of this dream, he started talking about his wife. Cordelia did not want to know about his wife. She wanted him to bang on her door in the middle of the night with his fist, to come in with a suitcase in his hand and call her by her name and say, 'I have come to live with you at my own peril.' She wanted him to carry her into a strange house and close the door. The doctor said his wife went to bed early, well before him. He said on fine nights he sat out on the step behind his house and smoked a cigarette. From there he could see the headland further up, see where the road curved down towards the lights of her village.

They gave each other things. That was their first mistake. He took a small pair of surgical scissors from his pocket and snipped off a lock of Cordelia's hair. He kept this lock of hair between the pages of a book named *Doctor Zhivago*. Another time, having lain out in the dunes past dark, they accidentally wore each other's scarves home. He gave her old books whose pages were edged in gold. And Cordelia wrote long, lavish letters on thick notepaper, pasted petals on the headings. In the middle of the night, while his wife and children slept, the doctor climbed high up above the drawing room, pushed the attic door open and placed the things she gave him under asbestos insulation between the joists. He knew they would be safe there, for his wife was afraid to climb.

But the doctor never wrote a line to Cordelia. When he went away to Lisbon on vacation with his wife, Cordelia received no word from him, not so much as a postcard. The only specimen of his handwriting she'd ever witnessed was when he gave her painkillers for an earache. Across the label in an almost illegible hand was written: One to be taken with water (or vodka) three times daily.

Cordelia is almost there. She passes concrete railings at the car park and climbs the steep incline up, up through the dunes, under the shadow of the mountain. She stands to get her breath back, watches the toss and turn of the blue-bellied tide breaking into perpetual, salty lather on the strand. Reeds are bending low to let the wind pass. There's little to show human presence; the wind has rubbed all footprints from the sand. Just a broken plastic spoon, the wrapper off a choc-ice, a buckled beer-can, a child's beaded purse. Cordelia stops and stoops to pick it up, but it's empty, its lining torn.

Lights from the town throw an orange sash across the

east. She hears music, travellers playing Jim Reeves records in the halting site, the systematic purr of a generator. A piebald mare whinnies and canters down along the ocean's edge as if she too has dreamt of a man holding a gun to her head. Clouds accumulate, thicken into darkness. Cordelia finds the mossy patch upon the hill where they first sat down ten years ago. She lies down in the reeds, pulls her collar close around her throat, and listens. She remembers the sound of his car, the veins of his wrist, the wind singing.

The doctor's wife climbed up into the attic. He entered his drawing room one afternoon and found there on the floor the piece of black ribbon he'd taken from Cordelia's hair to bundle up her letters, each one addressed to his surgery and marked 'strictly confidential'. When he raised his head, he saw legs dangling over the edge of the manhole. They were the muscular, white legs of a tennis player, his wife's legs.

'Whose hair is this? Who sent these letters? Who have you been seeing? Who owns this ribbon? Who? I want to know; speak to me. I want to know. Who is Cordelia? Cordelia who?' The doctor kept his hands in his pockets while his wife read aloud from the pages. She began to cry. It was late afternoon when she began. He sat down in the armchair by the fire and through the window watched the shuddering rosebushes. She dropped each page to the living-room floor as she read. The pages floated on the air, cascading down towards the rug, and by the time she'd finished reading, she had asked for a torch to read by and the rug was littered with pages. At the end of many of these pages was written, in a generous hand, the name Cordelia. The doctor's wife would not come down. For a long time afterwards she sat there, insisting she would jump if the doctor would not tell her the truth.

'Are you in love with her?'

'No,' said the doctor.

'She's obviously in love with you.'

The doctor did not answer.

'Are you going to stop?'

'Yes.'

'Are you going to leave me?'

'Of course not.'

Eventually his wife was lured down. A splendid fire throve in the hearth, for the doctor, out of nerves, had thrown shovelfuls of coal on to the flames. Before dawn, in the presence of her husband, she slowly burned every one of Cordelia's letters. The doctor watched as fire devoured the pages, Cordelia's lock of milky hair singeing in the blue heat.

'She's a blonde,' said the doctor's wife and breathed deep the scent of another woman in the cashmere scarf before throwing it to the fire.

The doctor called Cordelia into his surgery and in a low, sensitive voice, informed her their affair was over. He joined his hands and pushed his thumbs round in small, anti-clockwise circles. This must be what it's like to be informed of a terminal illness, she thought. He talked and talked, but Cordelia had stopped listening. She was reading the eye-test chart behind his head. She could read down to the seventh line. Maybe she needed glasses.

But then the doctor's voice changed. He put his head in his hands.

'Oh Cordelia,' he said. 'I can't leave my wife.'

'How romantic.'

'You know I can't leave. Think of the children. Think of them asking, "Where's Daddy?"'

'Would you leave if you hadn't children?'

'Wait for me,' he said. 'In ten years' time the children will be grown and gone. Promise you'll meet me on New Year's Eve at the turn of the century. Meet me that night and I will come home and live with you,' he said. 'I promise.'

Cordelia laughed outrageously and that was the last she saw of him. She passed patients in the waiting room; was everyone waiting for this man? The snivelly middle-aged woman with the tissues, the pale man with his bandaged arm, the wounded.

Gradually, the bad dream faded. The green curtain and the window furled backwards into memory, but the promise stoked like a bright blade in Cordelia's head. Cordelia coveted her solitude. She started reading late into the night, playing her piano, practising uncomplicated airs. She talked to herself, speaking disjointed sentences freely in the empty rooms. Slowly Cordelia became a recluse. She covered the TV with a tablecloth and put a vase of flowers there; she threw the transistor radio away. She made lists, paid her bills through the mail. She got the phone in, realised the turfman, the grocer, the gasman, anyone she wanted, would call round and deliver. They left the cardboard boxes, the gas cylinders outside the house, took the cheques from under the stone. She rose late, drank strong tea, made a ritual of cleaning out the grates. She stopped attending mass. Neighbours knocked on her door and peered in through the windows, but she did not answer. A powder of rust-coloured ash fell over the house, accumulated on the sills, the curtain rails. It seemed that every time she moved she raised dust.

Evenings, she lit the fire, watched the whoosh of flame around the turf, and listened to the rhododendron hedge, the leaves of the Virginia creeper rubbing against the window panes. Cordelia imagined someone out there in the dark, licking a finger, a thumb, rubbing a peep-hole in the dirty glass to see in, to see her, but she knew it was the hedge. She had always kept the garden, stayed out in summer with the clippers, trimmed it all back and raked the ear-like laurel leaves off the sandy path, mowed the grass, lit small, inoffensive fires whose smoke poured down beyond the clothes-line. The neglected hedge began to intrude upon the house, grew so thick and close that all the downstairs rooms loomed in constant shadow, and when the sun was going down, strange, monkey-puzzle shadows poured into the sitting room. Cordelia could sit under the light of the reading lamp in daytime and pretend it was night. Time altered, took on unfathomable dimensions. Sometimes, when the weather was warm and the rhododendron buds opened, she walked naked around the sheltered house, brushing against the smooth, damp leaves, the swollen blooms, and petals fell around her feet. Nobody ever saw her.

Hunchbacked clouds slide across the headland at Strandhill, grey-dull clusters gathering momentum out along the cliffs while behind them night discharges darkness. A mossy parchment with a view of the sea. Nothing and everything has changed. Cordelia feels tired. She feels that she has run a very, very long race and now her heartbeat is slowing down to normal. She puts her hand up to her face, takes comfort in her hot breath. She feels the wind dying, the slop of ocean on the strand. She pulls her coat around her, fastens up the buttons. She waits. Not long now. She closes her eyes, remembers rhododendron petals falling, pale pink blooms and grass, damp, long grass, beneath her feet. The snip, snip of a hedge clipper, his scissors cutting her hair, hot, broken sleep, a green bruise fading on her neck, fallen apples, his hand winding her hair, the pale man in the waiting room.

She wakes to the sound of a small parade, people marching across the hill, holding torches, gearing up for midnight. Brass, trumpet music. A boy in costume beating a drum. They march in their own time. Girls in miniskirts, twirling batons, making for the lights of town.

'Cordelia.' The woman to whom the voice belongs stands over her, keeping her hands hidden. 'You don't know me. I believe you knew my husband; he was the doctor,' she says.

Was the doctor? Was?

'I have come here to tell you that the doctor won't be coming.'

Cordelia says nothing. She just sits there and listens.

'You didn't think I knew?'

The doctor's wife is a lithe, small woman with lots of white in her eyes. She pulls the belt of her raincoat tight around her waist as if to make it smaller. 'It was obvious. When your husband comes home from house-calls with sand in his shoes, his shirt-buttons done up wrong, hair brushed, smelling of mints, and a gigantic appetite, a wife knows.' She takes out a pack of cigarettes and offers Cordelia one. Cordelia shakes her head, watches the woman's face in the flame of the lighter. Heart-shaped face, short eyelashes, a determined chin.

'You write nice letters.'

A drum is beating on the headland.

'You know the funniest thing?' the doctor's wife says. 'The funniest thing is, I used to pray he'd leave me. I used to get down on my knees and say one Our Father and ten Hail Marys and a Glory Be for him to leave me. He kept your letters and things in the attic; I used to hear him up there at night, getting the ladder. He must have thought I was deaf. Anyway, I was sure he'd leave me when I discovered them, when he walked in. If it's any consolation, he was in love with you. I'm sure of that. I didn't have the heart to leave him, nor him me. We were cowards, you see. It's a damned tragedy.'

She looks out towards the ocean and composes herself.

'Look at your hair. Your hair's white. What age are you?'

'Not yet forty.'

The doctor's wife shakes her head, reaches out to touch Cordelia's hair.

'I feel like I'm a hundred,' says Cordelia.

The doctor's wife lies down on her back in the reeds and smokes. Cordelia feels no ill-will towards this woman, none of the biting envy she imagined.

'How did you know I would be here? Nobody knew, only he and I. And I thought it absurd when he first asked me to wait.'

'He has a terrible memory, writes everything down. And he believes his handwriting is illegible. You're pencilled in. "C. Strandhill at midnight."'

'Strandhill at midnight.'

'Not very romantic, is it? You'd think he would remember something like that.'

The parade drifts into town. The travellers have lit a fire in the car park. There's a smell of burning rubber and then the doctor runs up the dunes, breathless and smiling until he sees his wife.

'I took a wild guess,' says the doctor's wife.

He stands there, looking ten years older, looking at Cordelia. In the moonlight, his suit is shiny. He is alive and it is almost midnight. Cordelia is pleased, but nothing is as she imagined. The doctor, stiff with shock, does not reach out for her. He does not lie down in the tall grass and put his head in the crook of her arm as he used to. He stands there as if he has arrived too late at the scene of an accident, knowing he might have done something if only he had come earlier. Behind their backs the perpetual noise of the ocean folds in on itself. Together they listen to the tide, the waves, counting down what time remains. Because they don't know what to say or do, they do and say nothing. All three of them just sit there and wait: Cordelia, the doctor and his wife, all three mortals waiting, waiting for somebody to leave.

Where the Water's Deepest

The au pair sits on the edge of the pier this night, fishing. Beside her, cheese she salvaged from the salad bowl at dinner, her leather sandals. She removes the band from her ponytail and shakes her hair loose. Leftover smells of cooking and bathsuds drift down from the house through the trees. She slides a cube of cheese on to the hook and casts. Her wrist is good. The line makes a perfect arc in the air, drops down and vanishes. Slowly she reels it towards her, where the water's deepest. She's caught a nice perch this way before.

Lately she's not been sleeping well, wakes to the same dream. She and the boy are in the yard at evening time. Wind bloats the clothes on the line and black trees are nuzzling overhead. Then the ground trembles. Stars fall and jingle around their feet like coins. The barn roof shudders, lifts off like a great metal leaf, scraping clouds. The earth fractures open and the boy is left standing on the other side.

'Jump! Jump, I'll catch you!' she yells.

The boy is smiling. He trusts her.

'Come on!' She holds her arms open wide. 'Jump! It's so easy!'

He runs fast and jumps. His feet clear the canyon, but

then the strangest thing happens: her hands melt and the boy drops backwards into the darkness. The au pair just stands on the edge and watches him fall.

Sometimes she dreams this twice in the same night. Last night she got up and smoked a cigarette in the bathroom and watched the moon. The light slid off the gold-plated taps, dipped into the porcelain sink, making shadow. She brushed her teeth and went back to bed.

That afternoon they'd dug up worms and carried their fishing gear down to the lakeshore. The au pair flipped the boat right-side-up and slid it into the water, held it steady for the boy. 'Right-ho!' she said and rowed them out past the shade of the pier. The boy was wearing a Salt Lake City baseball cap his father had brought back from a business trip. Freckles had grown together across his nose; the scab on his knee was healing. His hand dangled over the side and tore the water's surface as she rowed. When she raised the oars and let them drift, mosquitoes gathered quickly in a small cloud around the boat.

'Do they have bugs in the Reef?' the boy asked.

The au pair's voice changed when she talked about home. She talked as if she could reach out through the past and touch it with her hands. She baited his pole, told him how she'd learned to scuba-dive and snorkel with a spear, explored the hidden world under the ocean. Gigantic mountains where the fish swam in schools and changed direction all at once. Seaweed swirling. A turtle with great spirals on his back, swimming past. Seahorses.

'I wanna go scuba-diving here,' the boy said.

'We can't, love. Your lake's too dark and muddy; the bottom isn't sandy like the ocean, it's mud. Mud deeper than two grown men standing one on top of the other. Way too dangerous for diving.'

The boy turned quiet for a while. Quarter horses in the meadow whinnied and cantered down the hill, snorted to a stop at the water's edge.

'Let's play "What's-it-like?"' she said and slapped a bug on her arm.

The boy shrugged. 'Okay.'

She went first: 'This boat is like one half of a big Brazil nut.'

'Your head is like a cabbage.'

'Your eyelashes are the colour of a palomino's mane.'

'What's that?' the boy asked.

'A horse. I'll show you a picture some time.'

'I've eyes like a horse?'

'Your turn.'

'Your farts are like baked beans.'

'Your farts are like deadly silences,' she said.

'You're like a mama,' he said, and looked into her eyes.

'Speaking of mamas,' she said, 'your mama should be back soon. We better get on home.' She gripped the oars and rowed them to the shore.

Easter is coming. Before dinner they sat on rugs in the

den and made cards out of thick, expensive paper his mama bought downtown and called each other partner: 'Merry Easter, partner. Eat lotsa eggs,' his card read. She held his hand, wrote the letters for him, but he told her what to write. He drew the 'X's on the bottom by himself. On the front, in crayon, he drew two stick figures on a brown background.

'What are those?' his father asked. A big, red-haired man with Irish ancestors and eyes an unrelenting shade of blue. He was smoking a cigar, watching CNN with his feet up.

'Scuba-divers,' the boy said.

'I see.' His papa smiled. 'Come here, son.'

The boy rose and climbed up on his father's lap.

'Take a break, sweetheart,' the man told the au pair.

She got up. She passed the dishes in the kitchen sink, walked out into the night and slammed the door.

Down at the lake the au pair hears the toilet flush, then the swash of bathwater in the pipes. Bedtime. The boy's mama, a tall, blonde woman with high cheek-bones who runs a real-estate agency downtown, always puts the boy to bed. That is the arrangement. She bathes the boy, reads *Green Eggs and Ham* or *Where the Wild Things Are*. His mama is well educated. Sometimes she reads from a book of poems by Robert Frost and plays Mozart on the stereo. Later, the au pair will go in and see if the boy is still awake, kiss him goodnight.

*

Last winter they travelled north, a three-hour flight to New York City for a long weekend. They stayed in a hotel suite nineteen floors up with a small balcony and a view of Manhattan. That evening the boy's mama dressed up in a loose silk dress and a mink jacket, took her husband's arm and they went out to dinner. The au pair ordered a pizza funghi and Coca-Colas from room-service, played snakes and ladders with the boy. He threw the dice, and they climbed and slithered up and down the board till bedtime. The au pair stayed up, took a hot shower and wrapped herself in the fluffy dressing gown with the hotel crest impressed on the lapel. She opened the balcony door and from the arm-chair watched the skyline, the evening bleeding into darkness behind the tallest buildings; but she didn't dare go out and look down. Instead she wrote letters home, saying she might not be back for Christmas after all, how she missed the ocean, but they were good to her; she wanted for nothing.

It was late when they got back. She'd dozed off in the chair, but woke to hear them talking in the bedroom. Then the talking stopped and the man went out on to the balcony. Cigar smoke and freezing cold air drifted back into the room. He bolted the balcony doors and came back in and sat on the edge of the couch looking down at her. He smelled of beer and Polo aftershave and the au pair felt the cold off his good wool suit.

'You know what happens if we lose the baby, don't you?' he said. 'We lose the baby, we lose the babysitter.

You keep those balcony doors locked, sweetheart, or you'll be taking the first plane home.' He kissed her then, a strange, deliberate kiss, an airport kiss for someone you're glad to see the back of, then got up and went back in to his wife.

When she heard his snores, she rose and stepped out on to the balcony. A weak wind was driving large snowflakes across the air, sifting them into flurries. A December speckled night with the hooting of traffic. Soon it would be Christmas. She gripped the railings and looked down. A snarl of angry yellow taxis clotted the intersections on the streets below. She sucked her breath in. She remembered reading somewhere that a fear of heights masks an attraction to falling. Suddenly that made some kind of terrifying sense to her. If she didn't think of jumping off, standing on the edge wouldn't cost her a thought. She imagined falling, imagined how that might feel, to dive down, be lost like that, mean everything for moments only, then be gone. She backed inside and locked the doors.

The next morning they planned to visit F.A.O. Schwarz Toystore. In the lobby, the au pair wrote the boy's name and his room number on a slip of paper and pinned it to the inside of his trouser pocket.

'Now give this to the nice policeman if you get lost.'

'But I won't get lost!' he said.

'Of course you won't.'

It is dark now down at the lake. The au pair senses

movement in the bushes at the far bank. Somewhere in those fields are wild boars. Once the boy's father trapped a boar, paid a man to slaughter the animal and stacked the deep-freeze solid. Another dozen casts or so and she'll turn in. The cheese is nearly used up anyhow. She listens to the frogs ribbuting and for some reason remembers the tock, tock of the electric fence back home. Her father taught her never to touch it with the palm, always the back of the hand; that way the reflex would make her pull away, not grip it if the current was still running. Small things, that's what fathers are for, far as she can see. Practicalities. How to tie your shoelaces and buckle your seat belt. She reels in the line and checks the bait, casts again. The bait plops, but she can no longer detect the line against the sky.

Nobody sees the boy leave the house. He sneaks down the back steps but doesn't hold on to the railing like he's told. It doesn't matter that his eyes have not adjusted to the darkness; he knows the grassy slope that leads down to the lake. He can see her pale blouse, the sleeve coming up, the elbow whipping back, casting. The boy runs although he is told never to run near water. Small grunts, like the noises his cousin's doll makes when he turns her upside-down and right-side-up again, come from his chest. The au pair has her back to him. The boy's feet are soundless; he is silent as a panther in the cool grass.

The au pair doesn't turn her head until his foot hits the first plank of the pier.

[45]

'Yoo-hoo! Catch me! Catch me!' the boy calls.

He is running, fast. The rod drops from her hands. The boy's foot catches on something and then he seems to travel a long, long way. The au pair is finding her feet, trying to stand and turn all at once. The boy feels a chill. Suddenly her arms are there, enfolding him as he knew they would. He flops down and giggles on her shoulder. 'Surprise!' he yells.

But she isn't laughing.

The boy goes silent. Beyond the safety of her shoulder, he detects danger. Beyond her, nothing. Only deep, black water and beneath it the world of soft, velvet mud. Mud deeper than two grown men.

'Oh, my baby,' the au pair whispers. 'There, there.' She rocks him and he rests his head on her shoulder for a long, long time, feeling her chest fall and rise. She kisses the silk of his hair; his eyelashes brush against her collarbone. The au pair holds him until their heartbeats slow and a woman's voice calls out the boy's name. Then she carries him back up to the lighted house and gives him to his mama.

The Ginger Rogers Sermon

Don't ask me why we called him Slapper Jim. My mother stamped his image in my head, and I was at an age when pictures of a man precede the man himself. The posters verify: Thin Lizzie with a V of chest exposed, Pat Spillane's legs racing across my bedroom wall, the ball poised. I was the girl with the sweet tooth and a taste for men. And pictures.

I have a photographic memory. I can see every tacky page of my cousin's wedding album, the horseshoe on the cake with the man slightly taller than the woman and their feet stuck in the frosting. I parcel out my life in images the way other people let the calendar draw a line around them every month. That time of Slapper Jim was the time of the strangest pictures.

We killed pigs around then, ate pork cracked in its own fat with a pulpy sauce. Plasticine-grey and apple-green, those were the colours of my home. Ma held my dinner plate with the tail of her skirt and talked through her day while I tucked in:

'You should see the new lumberjack your da hired. Slapper Jim, they call him. A great big fella he is! Walked in here and I'll tell ya nothing but the truth, he leaned up against the partition there and I thought the whole yoke was going to cave in.'

My brother, Eugene, quacks his hand behind her back. I spear a slice of pork and in my mind see a giant, the earth tremoring where he walks. A man who doesn't know his own strength. That can be dangerous. I've seen my father crack a cow's ribs with his fist, just trying to slide her over in the stall.

'I gave him his bit of dinner and he was able to reach over for the handle on the saucepan without getting up. Ate eleven spuds. Eleven spuds if ya don't mind! Yer lucky there's aer a one left.'

Ma rummages in the cutlery drawer for a spoon. Tapioca and stewed apples, I suppose. I hope for sherry trifle, gooey caramel, dollops of ice-cream.

'What's for afters?'

They leave me alone here on Saturday nights. Eugene goes too, even though he doesn't dance. Him staying home with me is a sissy thing to do because he's so much older. Seven years older. I was made out of the last of my father's sperm. I found that out just recently. My mother says I am The Accident in the family. My father tells people I am The Shakings of the Bag, which I suppose is much the same thing.

Dance mad, my parents. Ma says a man who can't dance is half a man. She's taught me the harvest jig and the waltz, the quickstep and the Siege of Ennis in the parlour. She says dancing is good therapy, makes her feel like she's in time with the world. Mostly we move where we're put, stooping under the rain and such, but dancing frees her up, oils her joints, she says. Everyone should know how to move in their own time. She puts the record on, I shake Lux across the lino, and we whirl around the parlour floor like two loonies. I am the man loony. I pretend I don't see her watching her reflection in the mirror of the sideboard as we pass. The Walls of Limerick requires two-facing-two, so we hold our hands out to imaginary partners and move them into the places they should go. I like this, knowing what Ma will do, where she'll go before she does, not having to think about it.

Saturdays smell of girls: wet wool, nail-polish and camomile shampoo. In the kitchen, Ma sets her hair. We call it The Salon. I hold the pins between my lips and roll her hair around the spiky curlers, stiffen it with setting lotion. Her head goes into the net and she sits in under the hood of the dryer we bought down at the auction when the His 'n' Hers went out of business. I hand her an old *Woman's Weekly* and imagine it's *Vogue*. The last page is ripped out so Da can't read about women's problems.

'Do you want a coffee!' I shout above the noise.

There was never any coffee in that house. She stays under there, deaf and talking loud like an old person, and I hand her a cup of frothy Ovaltine and an hour later she's out, relieved and pink. Then the daubs of shoe-cream, the shush of the steam iron smoothing out the creases. The shuffle of the entertainment pages and

Da working a lather for his face, sticking the headlines on his chin to stop the blood. Ma wriggling into her flesh-coloured roll-on, big elastic knickers to keep her belly in. Pot Belly, I call her:

'Are ya going dancing now, Pot Belly? Where's the beauty contest, Pot Belly? Where did yer pot belly go, Pot Belly?'

She calls me The Terror: 'Shut up, ya terror.' She dots Lily of the Valley behind her ears with the glass stopper and slides her tapping feet into her dancing shoes, ready to take off.

'You won't fall into the fire, now will ya?' Da always having the last word, jingling his keys like they belong to the only car in the parish.

'No, Da.'

Eugene pulling on his corduroy jacket, giving me a look like I shouldn't be alive.

The film comes on after the nine o'clock news. I change into my pyjamas and find the biscuits. She hides them in the washing machine or the accordion case or the churn. Once Eugene ate them all and left a note that said: 'Find a better hiding place next time,' but Pot Belly went mad, so now we leave nothing and she says nothing. That's the way it is in our house, everybody knowing things but pretending they don't.

I turn off all the lights and sit with my feet up and play with myself in the dark and hope the actors take off every stitch and go skinny-dipping in close-up. *The Birds* is the name of tonight's film. Birds line up on the wires, watching the children with their glassy eyes. Ready to swoop. Even the teachers can't offer them protection. I think of the grey crows picking out our ewes' eyes. I hear a noise but it's only the milk strainer hammering the glass in the wind. Looks like a metal claw, a wiry hand. I slide the bolt across the door and let the setter up on the couch. I keep my eyes shut when the birds dive on the town.

It's after midnight when the headlights cross the room. Ma wobbles in, opens the fridge, its light shining pink on her cheeks. Da slides the kettle over on the hotplate and warms his hands, ready for a feed.

'Saw the Slapper down in Shillelagh. He was out on the floor with a one.'

'And the size of her,' Ma chips in. 'No bigger than a bantam hen she is, sitting up beside him. And neather one of 'em has a step in their foot. Fecking useless.' She bites into a tomato with a vengeance and Eugene heads for the stairs before she starts her Ginger Rogers sermon.

'How's the bantam?' is the first thing I say when I meet Slapper Jim. He laughs a big, red laugh that sounds like the beginning of something. He has plump lips and blonde hair and standing beside him is like standing in the shade. He's as big as a wardrobe. I want to open all his shirt buttons and look inside. 'Haw' is the word he uses all the time.

'Who's this bantam now, haw?' Sounds like he's talking down a well.

My father sits at the head of the table and rubs a wedge of tobacco between his palms and packs his pipe. He has no teeth to distract the smile away from his eyes.

'Ma says your one is like a bantam,' I say.

'Haw?'

'Do ya leave her sitting on the nest all week?'

'Maybe she's not nesting at all.'

'Pluck her.'

The bantam jokes went on until the end. The hatching, plucking, sideways-looking, gawky jokes carried us through summer and beyond.

Slapper doesn't wear a belt. When he pulls his trousers up, the hems don't reach his ankles. On real wet days, the men stay home and do odd jobs around the yard. They fence, pare sheeps' feet, weld bits and pieces. On Saturdays Eugene watches *Sports Stadium* and bites his nails. I help Slapper split the sticks. I am a girl who knows one end of a block from the other, knows to place it on the chopping block the way it grows, make it easier for Slapper. But I don't suppose it would make any difference. That axe comes down and splits it open every time, knots or no knots. Even the holly, which my father calls 'a bitch of a stick to split', breaks open under his easy strike. We have a rhythm going: I put them up, he splits them open. With other people, I take my hand away fast, but not with the Slapper Jim. He and I are like two parts of the same machine, fast and smooth. We trust each other. And always he gives his waistband a little tug when I'm putting them up, and that waistband slides down with every swing of the axe.

I too am a lumberjack in summer. Pot Belly says it is no job for a girl. Girls should flute the pastry edge or wash the car at best is what she thinks. I should tidy my room, practise walking around with a book flat on my head to help my posture. Anything to keep me home.

'Keep her away from the saws. If that girl comes home from that wood with no feet, don't come home here.'

We've all seen such things. Toes sawn off, an arm mangled in a winch, and once, a mare gone mad with the sting of a gad-fly pulling the slig out on to the road and scrapping the car. But when morning comes I'm up and ready, watching for Slapper's Escort in the lane.

Following the mare is the job for me. A grey Clydesdale with a white face, she's seventeen hands if she's an inch. And the smell of her, the warm earth smell like the inside of a damp flowerpot. I put my nose on her neck and breathe in. And she's smart too, knows to stop when she snags and bikes up without putting out your shoulder. No dirt in her, but still she'll lash your face with that tail if you're not quick. We're clear-falling every second line on the slopes. Slapper and Da fall and trim, Sitka spruce mostly, and larch, the trimmer's dream. I hook the chain around the slig and follow the mare down the lines on to the car-road, drawing the timber as close together as I can, keeping the butts even. I unhook the slig and lift the swing back up on the hames and then hold on to the mare's tail and let her pull me back up the line. Slapper says I have brains to burn, thinking of that. Da says I should give some to Eugene because he does nothing, only sit around on his arse with his nose in a book all day.

We drink mugs of tea from a flask at nosh-up, milk from an old Corcoran's lemonade bottle. Soda bread soggy with tomatoes and sardines in red sauce. The tea tastes bitter towards the end of the day. Slapper dents the bumper where he sits, talks with his mouth full.

''Uckin 'lies,' he says when he swats the flies. They light on the horse-dung and the jam. They chase me up and down the lines and drive the mare cuckoo. I sit on the mare backwards with my feet up on her flanks while she grazes the bank, and wait for somebody to open the biscuits. Slapper lifts me up there. 'Peaches,' he calls me, but I am nothing like a peach. My father says I'm more like a stalk of rhubarb, long and sour.

'Ya have a way with that baste, Peaches. She bites the arse off me.'

'It's always hanging out anyway, Slapper. Here,' Da says, handing over a wad of baling twine, 'until ya buy yerself a belt.'

'Haw?' Slapper smiles, but he doesn't tie his trousers up. He just looks at the twine in a way that makes Da put it back into his pocket, and gives his waistband a tug the way another man might push his glasses up on his nose.

Slapper teaches me the tricks of the trade. He holds his big finger up but doesn't stoop when he says these things: 'Don't open the slig until you've unhooked her;

if she takes off, yer fingers will be dogmate. Don't stand in front of the saw; if there's a loose link and the chain breaks, you're fucked.' He opens up that forbidden world of adult language and invites me in. Then he leaves me alone to be capable.

We stay at it until dusk. Foresters come around with their kettles in the evenings and paint the stumps with the pink poison. We hide the saws and the oil and petrol cans under the tops up the line and let the mare loose in the field down the road. Every week the lorries drive up with their robot claws and load up the lengths. Twenty-five tons is a load for them, a cheque for us, and a pound of wine gums and a *Bunty* and *Judy* after mass and two choc-ices and gob-stoppers for me.

'What do they learn ya in school?' Slapper asks as we're driving the mare down to the field.

I know trigonometry. 'I know that the square on the hypotenuse is equal to the sum of the squares on the other two sides.'

'What's a highpotinhuze?' Jim pushes back the passenger seat to make room for his legs, but his knees are snug against the dashboard. He holds the mare's reins out through the open window as she trots next to the car. 'Go on, ya lazy cunt ya! Whup! Whup! Ya hairy, farting fucker ya. Go on!' He claps the outside of the door with his left hand.

'The child, Slapper. The child!' Da admonishes.

Slapper looks back at me. My father's eyes watch me in the rear-view mirror, but I pretend I haven't heard a word.

'What's this highpotinhuze?'

Those are the pictures from that time. Three dirty lumberjacks sligging out timber, the wood slick and white beneath the bark. The forester looking at me because I'm a girl. Eating packets of Bourbon Creams, spitting, listening to Radio One in the car when it rains, sharpening chain, files grinding on the rakers, the cutters shining all round like some deadly necklace. Slapper asking what they learned me in school, his file sharpening smack-on with the slant of the cutters every time. Da says Slapper's a great man with a saw. The last fella Da had working with him slid a matchstick in between the spark-plug and the petrol tank so she wouldn't start, but Da found out and gave him his walking papers. I tell Slapper Jim the things I learn in school. I know that Oliver Cromwell told the poor people 'To hell or to Connaught' (I can see him on his black horse, pointing west), that Jesus lost his temper. I can recite William Blake:

> *Tyger Tyger, burning bright,*
> *In the forests of the night;*
> *What immortal hand or eye,*
> *Could frame thy fearful symmetry?*

I can see it on the page, the curve of the question mark at the end. Slapper holds my hand and stands me up on the bonnet of the car in the rain, telling me to say the poems. I read them off my memory. He asks me what 'immortal' means, but I don't know. He says I am the morbidest child in Ireland.

'Get that child in out of the rain!' Da putting a damper on it from the driver's seat. 'Do ya hear me, Slapper? She'll catch her end and you can be the one to bring her home!'

But Slapper just smiles. 'Say the poems, Peaches.'

I shoot up like the rhubarb stalk Da says I am and the transformation begins. I take an interest in my cousin's old dresses. Flowery things with thin, patent belts and matching pointy shoes that pinch my toes. I limp home from school and make the announcement. Ma says 'Shusssssh!' and gives me the elastic belt and towels to catch the blood. I think it's the equivalent of Da's news-paper for his chin.

'Don't let yer father see them,' she says. Her always hiding women away, like we're forbidden.

Now that I am thirteen, I am sectioned off from men. It happens in school too, in gym class. I play basketball and jump over hurdles and come back all red-faced and sweaty and talk non-stop in class. Nobody sits beside me because I smell like an afterbirth. I wear the pads and Lily of the Valley and go dancing down the pub. Slapper Jim is always there with the bantam. I waltz around in the cigarette smoke with old men my father knows. Watch Sam Collins prancing across the floor in his patent shoes, swinging Pot Belly around, and him with his left hand up so high she can barely reach it. Foxy, we call him, with his head of slicked-back, silver hair, his horse's eye. The men's hands grip me by the waist and swing me round, same as I'm a bucket of water. They hold me close as an excuse not to let me go. The backs of their shirts are wet. I drink Babychams out of long-stemmed glasses. They taste like ice-cream and soften the pictures. Eugene sits with his elbows on the bar, watching the dancers, his shoe tapping in perfect time on the rung of his stool, but he won't get out on the floor.

Slapper cannot dance. If his feet move on the beat, it's an accident. He just doesn't catch the rhythm. He takes me out on to the floor and puts his arms around me and shifts his weight from one leg to the other, taking huge strides for the waltz. My head comes up to the fourth button on his shirt. I could almost see past him if I stood on my toes. I can smell him, get the whiff of the sticks on his chest as if he sweats out resin. Reminds me of the mare, the hair and the warmth under his shirt, the big feet moving over the floor. I try to lead him into the rhythm, exaggerating my sways, but he does not feel the music and I wind up stepping on his toes.

'Should have worn me steel toe-caps,' he says.

His bantam isn't even as tall as me, a dark, plump woman with a mouth like his. She wears a royal-blue blouse with gold sequins blown across the bust. He could scrape her sequins with the buckle on his trousers, if he had a buckle. That's how funny-looking they are.

At closing time, the couples stand outside, the women with their backs against the gable wall, the men leaning against them, both hands against the bricks, kissing. Snogging, we call it at school. I want to see Slapper snogging the bantam. I don't know why, but I want to see what that looks like. I think he'd have to lift her up on a beer barrel. I look for them, but they're never there at the gable wall. I wonder what it would be like to kiss Slapper, to have his strong hands inside my dress and his mouth on my mouth. Ma puts her arm around my shoulders and leads me to the car, shielding out that world of romance and men and women touching.

The winters are dark here. I shiver from the chill behind the curtains, squat without touching the toilet seat. Downstairs the paraffin-oil heater throws shapes like tears on to the kitchen ceiling. Ma turns up the wick, making the shapes dance when Slapper comes in. I think of the way she turns up the oven when she puts the second loaf in. She braids my hair in two long plaits while I eat spaghetti hoops and a fried sausage. She wets her thumbs on her tongue, catching up the stray hairs. I listen to the suck of Slapper's pink mouth slurping tea, the cast-iron pot with the Star of Bethlehem swinging on its hinge outside the window. I don't want to go to school.

I crack wafer ice on the puddles in the lane and smoke twigs until the bus comes, blow my breath out white. I bring home nits from school. Da holds me down with his farmer's grip while Ma douses my head with turpentine-smelling lotion. She pulls the comb along my scalp and catches the nits between the teeth and crushes them with a crunch beneath her thumb-nail on the kitchen table saying, 'There, we've got him.'

*

The snow has come this Saturday. I have taken every-thing but the blinkers off the mare, left the men to pack the gear. I am riding her the whole way home to keep her in the stable until the weather improves. When the car passes me on the road, the mare whinnies and trots on after them, but soon we are left behind. Slapper's hand waves from the passenger window. Sometimes you'd think he was the Pope or somebody. The road is quiet, but the mare's ears are up. Then further on I see three yearling colts leaning up against a field gate, wait-ing. I try to pull the mare to the far side of the road, but there's no bit in her mouth and it's impossible. She puts her nose to theirs, and squeals. I dismount. The colts have their willies out, the pink-and-black hoses almost reaching their girth lines. They snort and push the gate until I think it will fall over on to me. The mare kicks out with her hind leg and squats to piss on the road. I pull the reins down hard, but she is oblivious to me now. Her snorts deepen and the colts bite each other, their mouths fast and open. They scrape the bars with their hooves. I throw stones at them and eventually they launch into a farting gallop down the field and back again, trotting inside the ditch beside the mare as I pull her home. I am afraid to mount her until I get well away from the colts, knowing she will canter back given the slightest chance.

When I reach home, Slapper's grey Escort is still parked in the yard. He comes out of the barn and pulls me down into his arms.

'Are ya frozen, Peaches?' he says.

'She's horsing, Slapper!' My teeth chatter and my hands are stiff.

'Haw?'

'I'm not joking ya. Them colts nearly climbed over the gate to get at her.'

Slapper says nothing but smiles as he pours oats into her trough. We walk across the frozen mud towards the house. Pot Belly has made beef stew with the bone from the round steak sitting in the soup, dumplings bobbing on the surface. Eugene's reading a book called *Seven Deadly Nights at the Edge of the Universe*. His eyebrows have grown together since the last time I looked at him. Pot Belly gives out and tells Slapper he's not to be going home in this weather. He is to stay the night and she'll not hear otherwise.

Upstairs we make up the extra bed.

'I hope the shagger doesn't snore and keep me and Eugene up all night.' I say this to put her off the track.

'Your mouth's getting worse, young lady. I'll have to have a word with Slapper about that.'

But she never would. She, like the rest of us, thought the sun shone out of Slapper's arse.

He doesn't know I'm watching. He stands where the slant of blue light partitions the room. I am glad of the snow. Slapper closes the door behind him and doesn't bother to open the buttons on his shirt. Instead, he holds the back of his collar and pulls it over his head. There's hair all over his chest; his stomach is a plank of muscle.

He slides the zip down, exposes his legs, sits down, pulls the waistband down over his feet. I imitate Eugene's breathing in the far bed. Slapper comes over to my bed in his navy-blue underwear. He bends down over me. His breath fans my face. I am just about to let him kiss me when I hear the creak of the other bed.

His feet hang over the end of the mattress. I know by the quiet that the snow is still coming down outside. The light gets whiter. We are safe inside the drifts. Snowed in. Tucked up. Perhaps the drifts will come and he will have to stay another night.

'Are ya asleep, Slapper?' I whisper it.

'Haw?' For a long time he says nothing. 'It's a cold fucking house.'

I go to him, wrapped in my blankets. I pull his bed-clothes down and get in, compounding our warmth. I lie up against his back and breathe on the down of his neck. My hand slides around his waist, feels his hard belly, wanders shyly down through the curls of his pubic hair. I feel him stiffen. I think of the colts. When he turns over, his hands are cold. Big and gentle and precise. 'Jesus, Peaches,' I hear him whisper as his will subsides.

Three feet of snow has fallen over Ireland, the wireless says. I find a bonnet from an old Volkswagen and Slapper and I spend the afternoon sliding down the top field, right over the ditch, across the lane and into a nice curve in the field below. The track gets a little longer every time, but when we get off at the bottom and look back up, I cannot resist doing it again. Slapper pulls the bonnet in one hand and mine in the other and hardly says a word. Suddenly, I am somebody no one is supposed to know about.

I saddle the mare and take her the full circuit through the snow, down the lane and up past the bog-field. The moon brightens the dark sky like a fake sun, but the land is white. The world's turned upside-down. The evening is edged in blue like TV light. All the chainsaws have stopped. I listen to the puff of the mare's breath and her hooves compressing tracks along the snow. The smell of the pines is everywhere. We have just eased into a canter along the car-road when she shies. A pheasant flutters out over the trees. Horses frighten easily when there's wind. I pull her up and listen. It may be deer. I dismount and lead the mare down between the trees. The ground is dry, the moss smooth underfoot, and the mare stumbles. It's black beneath the branches. And then I get the smell. The mare pulls on the reins. I stop and listen. The wind pheews through the treetops, like someone learning to whistle. We walk towards the smell and then I see the source. Slapper's boots are there, neatly laced, his hems not reaching his ankles. His boots are at eye-level, beneath them nothing, nothing. As I draw closer, I see his face: his face is black and Christ, the smell. The wind spins him gently on the rope. I can't even cut him down. I leave him there, hanging in his own dung, and gallop home.

That was the hardest part, taking the others up there,

letting them see him like that. The way they stood and looked and cursed and said Jaysus and Holy Mother of Divine Jaysus and What in the name of Jaysus would a fine fella like him go and do a thing like that for? and took their caps off and carried him down the hill on the bonnet of the Volkswagen we had used as a sled, my father's coat draped over his body. Eugene standing there looking at me like I did it.

We come home from the wake and sit in the parlour. The room is like a second-hand furniture shop, the walls painted lime-green, a border of faded roses creeping below the ceiling. Pot Belly produces a bottle of Bristol Cream from the sideboard and fills four glasses to the brim. The padlock on the yard gate beats its clasp, hammering down the silence of the room. My father watches the sparks lifting into the soot. Eugene has no nails to bite; they are bloody at the quick. When his eyes meet mine, they are full of accusation and blame. I am aware of my own breathing.

Pot Belly brings candles down out of the kitchen, white, blessed candles she got at Easter, and lights them from my father's match. She stands them upright in their own grease and places them about the room. She takes a record from its sleeve and turns the light off. The room is lit by flame. On the mantelpiece stand trophies, silver-plated couples frozen in mid-swirl. They quiver in the firelight. The music starts. Pot Belly catches Eugene's hand and pulls him upright. He does not want to dance, but her tug is steady. I know what she is doing, and from my father's evasive eyes, that look he has when Ma is changing her dress, I know that something's going on, know my parents have spoken of this. They have it planned. Ma has always thought a man should know how to dance. The only flaw she could see in Slapper Jim was his leggy, graceless motion on the floor. She is teaching Eugene, as a precaution, as if him knowing these steps will carry him through, prevent him from tying a noose around his neck later on.

She begins the slow waltz and reluctantly he follows her, shifting his weight, his body stiff, his feet imitating hers. My father keeps his eyes on the fire. Pot Belly takes Eugene around the furniture, whispering one-two-three, one-two-three until the music stops. The stylus crackles in the groove and the rhythm changes to a quickstep. Da stands up, pulls off his overcoat and takes my hand. The steel of his suspender digs into my side. The voice of a travelling woman, clear and stern, pushes us together. Pot Belly counts the beats into Eugene's ear. One, one-two, one. We dance around each other, cautious of the space we're taking up. And then the song changes to a reel and there is nothing but the primitive da-rum of the bodhrán, the sound of wood pounding skin. Da-rum. Da-rum. The near screech of a fiddle, the pull of hair on string, the melodeon, the wheeze of bellows catching up, and the slight imprecision of the live instruments playing. We lift the furniture to the edge of the room, and I shake the Lux across the floor. We swig our drinks and exchange our partners. Eugene starts moving with the beat, throwing himself in time. Ma removes her shoes. Sweat darkens the back of my father's shirt. The music is raucous, ornamented. Our shadows are larger than we are, doubling our statures, bending us up on to the ceiling. It is two-facing-two. We face each other. Eugene jumps up and down like a high-land dancer and although he does not know the moves, he has found the rhythm. We move him into the places he should go. First the ladies exchange places, then the men. We take the man facing us and go right for seven and back again. We swing our partners and begin over. The fire heats the room and I take off my cardigan when the tune ends. Eugene and I gulp sherry. It tastes forbidden. Ma gets the stand from the hair-dryer and sings into it like it's a microphone. Eugene puts his hand up very high, imitating Foxy, sticks his belly out, and we move around in circles.

'Do ya come here often?' he says.

'I do when the ewes aren't lambing.'

'Do ya live in a disadvantaged area?' He belches.

'Yeah, I get the subsidy.'

'God, you're lovely. There's nothing like the smell of a hogget ewe.'

He breathes me in with his sherry breath. We move with the squeal and squeeze of the uileann pipes, we are pulled in with the bellows. The quavering lilt and sway of a tin whistle curls through the darkness. The long swath of hair that covers Da's bald patch falls down and almost touches his shoulder. Ma pulls off her roll-on and swings it like a hula hoop on her index finger, keeping her left hand at her waist. The last picture I remember is the roll-on flying across the room with the snap of elastic and Eugene asking, 'Can I interest you in a snog at the gable wall?' as he swings me in a perfect twist.

Storms

My mother dreamt things before they happened and found things in her dreams. That morning she came down all dreamy, sleepy, saying, 'I know where the old slash-hook is now.' She pulled her boots on and I followed her up the bog. She stopped under a sycamore, and pointed to where a clump of briars choked the limestone wall.

'It's in there,' she said.

And sure enough, she was right. We chopped through those briars with our new slash-hook and found the old.

The dairy was a dark, damp place my parents filled with the things they seldom used. From the time before me. Yellow paint bubbled on the walls and flagstones shone across the floor. Bridles hung stiff on the beams, their bits dusty. The churn was still there and the smell of the sour milk still in it, the wood smooth but riddled with woodworm, the paddles long since lost. I never remember glass in those windows, only rusted bars and the strange applause of the wind blowing in through the trees.

Someone shoved the old incubator and run in there too, a rusted, metal affair that used to shine like teaspoons. We would put new chickens in there, scoop

them up in our hands like yellow petals and drop them
into that heat, the fluffy balls with legs always moving,
taking in that warmth as their own. Warmth keeps us
alive. Sometimes those yellow moving balls fell down,
the cold outside winning over, the feet like orange
arrows pointing down. My father's hand chucked them
out like young weeds. My mother's picked them gently;
inspecting those yellow bodies for some sign of life, and
finding none, she'd say: 'My poor chicken,' and smile at
me as she slid them down the shoot.

The milk strainers were still there too, the old gauze
hanging in dirty clumps on a fraying thread. And the
jars of gooseberry jam that smelled like sherry, shrunken
in the glass with the whisker of mould. We used to make
crab-apple jelly, quarter those sour fruits and boil them
to a pulp, cores and seeds and all. Poured the lumpy
fluid into an old pillowcase, a corner on each leg of a
stool turned upside-down. Drip. Drip. Drip. Into the
preserving pot all night.

I went into the dairy when I was sent: for a pot of var-
nish, six-inch nails, a bridle for a mare whose head was
big. The latch was too high. I had to stand on a can of
creosote to reach up and the metal round I pressed on
was leaf-thin. When I went there of my own accord, it
was to look into the chest, a big metal, rusted box, a
pirate's suitcase to a child. So old that if you emptied it
out and held it up to the light, it would be like looking
through a colander. There was nothing in it I liked – old
books stuck together with damp, no pictures, brown

maps and some prayer-books. 'It all belonged to yer father's people,' my mother told me, using the voice he was not supposed to hear. The chest was just as long as me and half as tall, with a tight lid and no handles. I would open it and look at those things, finger the books with their fractured spines, the missing covers, slam the lid down hard, make that metal screech.

Then the dream came and changed everything. My mother dreaming of her mother, dead. Her wailing in the kitchen waking me in the middle of the night. Banging the kitchen table. Me standing in my turtle pyjamas at the end of the stairs, watching through the dark. My mother curling up on the floor, my father who never spoke a tender word, speaking tender words. Coaxing her, saying her name. Mary, Mayree, ah Maayree. The two people who never touched, whose fingers left the gravy jug before the other's clasp, touching. I crept back upstairs and listened as those tender words changed into something else.

Morning brought the telegram. My mother rolled it between her fingers like a cigarette paper. My father made arrangements. A neighbouring woman's hand slapped mine when it turned the wireless on. My grandmother, the woman with the purple rash patching her body, the old, blue-veined breasts sagging, the jaundiced skin we had washed like a painting, came home stiff in a frill-lined box and we put her in the cool of the parlour.

Neighbours came in a convoy after the funeral, cars

bumper-to-bumper in the lane. I sat on strangers' laps. They passed me around like the tobacco pouch and I drank three big bottles of lemonade. My aunt stood guarding the ham. 'Who's for another nice bit of centre cut then?' the carving knife deadly in her hand.

My mother sat staring into the fire and never said a word. Not even when the sheep-dog got up on the chaise longue and licked himself.

Mother took to cleaning out the cow-house, even though we sold the cows years back. She went out with the yard brush and the bucket, scrubbed the stalls, the aisle, even shone the old hubcap we used to pour frothy milk into for the cats. And then she'd come inside and speak to the statues until dinner-time. She imagined storms. Locked herself under the stairs when she heard wind, put cotton wool in her ears when the thunder came. Hid under the table with the dogs. Once my father and I, rolling barley in the loft, watched her calling up the field to the cows. 'Chuck! Chuck! Hersey! Chuck! Hersey!' Her rattling the handle on the zinc bucket to bring those imaginary cows down. My father gentled her indoors. And that was when she started living upstairs.

So when summer came, I was the one who carried out the big teapot to the men, the spout plugged with a page from *The Farmer's Journal*. The men sucked their tráithníns and watched me and told my father with full mouths that I would soon be old enough.

She came for me in the middle of the night, wearing a

powder-blue nightdress I had never seen before. She pulled me out of bed, down the stairs in the dark and out through the mown meadow, past the cocks of hay, our bare feet picking up the seed. Up and up we went through the stubble fields, her hand a vice grip. The tail of her nightie whipping out behind her in the wind. And then we reached the top of the top and laid down on our backs, watching the stars, she with her brassy hair and mad words, not senseless at all, but sensing what we couldn't. The way the dog hears the car in the lane first.

She pointed out what she called the saucepan, a bunch of stars huddled over the treetops, and told me how it came to be there. How animals parched with thirst had no water. Giraffes' necks bending with the drought, sheep losing wool, snakes' bodies too dry to bend; but a young sow found a saucepan full of water and gave them all a drink to tide them over until the clouds wrung themselves out. The saucepan had a crooked handle and when the animals had drunk, the stars took on its shape and that's what was up there. And I could see it too, joining the white dots in the sky, feeling the turtles on my pyjamas start to crawl along my legs, under my armpits.

We stayed there until dawn, the smell of hay coming up on the wind. Her telling me the way my father's hands bruised her for fifteen years, the difference between loving and liking somebody. How she didn't like me any more than him because I had the same cruel eyes.

That's when I started going into the dairy without reason. It was a quiet enough room, nothing only the wind and the gurgling of the water-tank overhead. The hole in the ceiling between the beams showed the babby-house, a place my sisters used to take their dolls and hit their heads on the sloping roof.

They were long gone the time the van came to take her away. My father said she was hurting, but it wasn't anything you could see. I asked him if he meant she was bleeding on the inside.

'Something like that,' he said.

I thought of the Sacred Heart picture over the sink, the red heart lit by the red light that never went out.

I open the metal chest and look inside. I pick up a prayer-book and finger the leaves. They are tan and smooth like my mother's arm. I open one of the torn, brown maps and, until I find a place I recognise, I cannot discern which is the land, and which the sea. The wing of an insect is stuck to Norway. I can hear my parents talking in the next room. I open another book and look for pictures, but there are none. I get into the chest, squat down. I hear glass breaking. The sound of what has become my mother's voice rises to a near-cry. Something falls. I pull the tin roof, let that metal fall in over me with a rusty, tightening screech. Everything turns black. It is as if I no longer exist. It is not me sitting on the damp books inside a big, black tin. The smell is old and musty like the smell in the bread-bin or the back of the cupboard where the cake-crumbs stay. A smell that's a cen-

tury old. I remember rats ate through the grid of the
incubator once. They got at the chickens and we found
pieces of fluff everywhere with legs attached, the fleshy
bodies eaten out. We found others terrified, exhausted
and hiding between cans of paint or rolls of sheepwire,
unable as yet to fly away. We picked them up, their yellow bodies throbbing, tiny bellows gone mad.

The last man who said I was old enough got scalded.
My mother always said there was nothing as bad as a
burn. And she was right. It's turning out that I'm taking
no nonsense from anybody. They leave their wellingtons outside the door now. And I haven't heard them
say the spuds are hard in the middle. I'd swat them with
the serving spoon. They know that too.

I visit her on Sundays, but she doesn't know where
she is or who I am.

'It's me, Mam,' I say.

'I never could stand the smell of fish,' she says. 'Him
and his herrings.'

'Do you not know me? It's Ellen.'

'Ellen of Troy! Get on yer horse!' she says.

She's a right hand at cards, cheats the other ones out
of their pocket-money every week and the matron has
to go and fish it out of her shoes while she's in the bath.

But I keep going back there to that loony bin. I like the
smell of disinfectant in the corridors, the nurses' rubber-
soled shoes, the quarrelling over Sunday papers. What
does that say about me? Mother always said madness

ran in families and I have it from the two sides. I suppose I've my own reasons for going there. Maybe I'm getting used to it. Just a little, taking a small share of it for my own protection. Like a vaccination. You have to face the worst possible scenario, then you'll be able for anything.

The Singing Cashier

Smethers, the postman, that greasy fuck with his brown letters. Here he comes in his proud-blue uniform. It's another day, another dense, bright space to blacken in. He strides up the street to our porch, slicks his hair back underneath his cap and talks in through the letter-box.

'Morning, girls!'

The voice is treacle-sweet, reaching down the hall as if to grope us. He lives next to a distant cousin of ours who owns a fresh-fish caravan up past the Mormon Road, brings us cod or lemon sole or whiting wrapped in newspaper.

'Yoo-hoo, ladies! Oh, girls!'

The stink of him. The come-and-get-me voice on him. Something's not right. We had fish three times last week. Fresh salmon once and this cousin's someone we hardly know, a woman with a van Mam mentioned.

'Yoo-hoo! Ladies!'

My sister Cora doesn't budge. She leans her elbow on the corner of the gas cooker and pulls on her morning cigarette, exhaling thin little beams of smoke. She never talks until that fag's stubbed out. Behind our kitchen wall the quick snorts of a knitting machine that wake us up continue. When our neighbours first moved in we thought it was him snoring, that their headboard was against our wall; but we were wrong. Here we do not know our next-door neighbours. Mam used to talk about neighbours. People playing poker until all hours, men raising a huge tent together for a marquee on the Square, pulling the ropes down tight around the stakes.

Cora takes a last pull, squashes out the butt and tightens the belt of her lilac dressing gown. I watch her bare footprints fade on the lino as she opens the door and lets him in.

'A vision in the mornings,' he says, his eyes starting at her bare feet and travelling up like she's something he could sketch. His lips are shiny with his own spit. 'Oh, the versatility of the postal system. The service! Where would you girls be without us?' He hands over the parcel, marches in, plomps his satchel down on the hallstand. A little rub of the hands, a glance round. 'Well, Cora, a cup a tea would be sweet.'

Rewards for the messenger.

My no-nonsense sister puts up with him. She needs his greasy parcels, I suppose, and cups of tea are cheap enough. She stares into the fridge, inventing breakfast. There's two eggs, a tub of Flora margarine, a wilted head of lettuce, the bright light showing up the emptiness. She shuts the door and plugs the kettle in. It's Wednesday and we're down to the last few teabags, so the cups will be peppered with dust today. Smethers sits down snug in the armchair. Cora turns on the radio, tunes into Jimmy Young who's giving things away.

Then she wriggles a coin out of her purse and hands it over.

'Will you go down and get me a box of matches?'

'Matches? But there's –'

'Piss off now, there's a love.'

She gives me the 'Just do it' look, so I stomp down to the newsagent's in Breswill Street, a good ten-minute walk each way, but I come home too soon and notice Smethers' belt is notched up tight and Cora's nightdress is inside-out, her hands fidgeting with the fuzz around her slipper. And the smell, like sleep gone sticky. Oatmeal boiled over.

Now I'm wise. I take my time. I dawdle to the shops and back, steal a bottle of milk from a blue door's step and sip it all the way into town, small creamy sips that thin down and get sickening towards the bottom. I buy a box of matches or whatever Cora asks for in the shops so we'll never have to talk. Through the jeweller's window I watch ladies trying on rings with big, precious stones, the Scottish assistant coaxing them up over their knuckles and prising them off again.

The wind accumulates in this town, cold gusts trapped by the rows of identical red-brick houses, some built in crescents like they're competing for the sunshine and the air. I stand out here among the pre-schoolers and the café women, sharing their gossip and ashtrays. Other girls my age are in school, wearing scratchy, plaid uniforms and swotting over O-Levels. I had enough of that and Cora didn't seem to mind, said it was up to me. I burned my schoolbooks slowly in a barrel out the yard, pages of algebra, home economics, continents curling up in flame and diminishing to ash. But now sometimes I miss it 'cos there's nothing else to do, nobody my own age, just the soaps and pay day and whatever brainwave Cora thinks up in the days before she gets her period.

Going home, I trail my hands along the railings until the railings disappear and the pavement gets uneven. Sometimes Smethers leaves the gate open and the dogs get in and cock their legs on the hydrangea, but I always wait in the porch and listen, just in case. Our porch is littered with warped plaster slabs, dried-out putty tins, things we never bothered to clear out after Dad.

Cora sings. She comes home from work and says, 'They're starting to call me the singing cashier down Tesco's. They're all saying how nice it is to hear somebody happy.'

'And are you?'

'Am I what?' she asks.

'Happy.'

'Happy? Happy?' She pats my head, and laughs. 'Put the kettle on, ya daft love.'

She drinks it black, holds the cup up close to her face and blows out small breaths against the steam. I love her like this. When she sits and thinks up ways to keep us safe from the outside world. Ways to keep this dingy house insulated from the coppers and the gasman, the TV licence woman with her sturdy little clipboard.

The photo of our father has fallen off the wall, but his frame leans against the skirting board, determined. It's a picture taken at Pembroke Dock with a trucker's meaty arm around each shoulder. A lorry-load of construction men packed up for the crossing and the duty-free. His eyes are dark and feisty. Neither one of us has bothered to replace the nail, to hang that bastard back up in our lives.

Upstairs, Cora showers, getting ready to go out with the other Tesco girls. She sings a song from her new Tori Amos album, her voice high and brittle as a boy's.

'Make sure the iron's not too hot!' she shouts down.

In rainy months like these we air our clothes by ironing them. Last time I scorched the backside of her polyester nightdress, leaving a triangular patch of brown. I don't like to think these things might be deliberate.

Outside, in a house opposite ours, lights come on; Japanese lanterns hang like fake moons in the windows. They are pretty shades of blush-pink and curd-yellow.

And that's the last good night of sleep we had because of what it said in the newspapers. Smethers comes early and uses the bell for once.

'Open up!'

Newspaper but no fish today. His cap is off and I think the distant cousin with the caravan must be dead. But it's worse than that. NIGHTMARE ON CROMWELL STREET, the headline reads. Cora sucks in breath and lights a Rothman's off the gas. Slowly, we take it all in. Young girls found under the floorboards. Buried in the garden. The happy couple with the heinous appetite arrested. Plans for an excavation.

The very first thought that comes into my mind is milk. That door was blue. I examine the unsuspicious terrace house in the photo, with number 25 hung in trellis on the dash, and then I know it's true: I drank Fred West's milk while my sister was fucking the postman.

My father knew him. Fred West came here, ate supper in our house. A brickie on the river side, his shoes were big and glossy black. A hairy man with a beard and dark eyebrows feeding into one another. Hairy. Like you'd have to blow on him to find out where his eyes were, but the papers show him clean-shaven with a reckless look, a savagery made noticeable by truth. I sat up on his lap and, united, we played against my sister in a game of drafts. I remember his big fingers clasping the pieces, jumping hers, doubling them into kings at the far side of the board and turning back again, taking more.

This morning Cora does not tell me to go out. Instead I am to put the kettle on. She leads Smethers down the hall, pushes his back against the wall. I hear her voice but not the words and a few minutes later he's slithering off down the street without a word, moving out of our lives. Finally he brought something she could not stomach. Those girls were my age. It could have been me. Cora sent me out to run fake errands on what must have been the most dangerous street in England so she could shag a man for the sake of a few fishy parcels. Suddenly I wish Mam was alive. I wish my mother was alive so Cora wouldn't have to mother me, feed me.

'That's the end of him,' she says, gathering up the paper again.

'I was tired of fish anyway. Maybe you'll shag a butcher next.'

She doesn't smile. Perhaps she cannot. She just sits under the window with her ankles tucked in under her backside and turns the pages of the newspaper. Behind her the sun is rising, gathering strength over the houses. In the morning light her hair looks dry and broken at the ends. She looks old today, not tired, but less ambitious, like somebody who's quit so she can move on.

I crack two eggs into the frying pan and watch their edges whiten.

'Dad knew him,' she says.

'Yeah.'

I tip the pan so the oil cooks the whites into a shape. Throw a couple of bread slices into the fat.

'They built that porch together. Jesus.'

'Hard or runny?' I say.

'What?'

'Your egg. Hard or runny?'

'Runny.'

She's looking at the photograph of Dad with his trucker friends. For a moment I think she may pick it up, but she doesn't. She looks down, continues to read the newspaper. She has my father's jaw, a squareness to her face I never noticed until now, determination, but her eyes say otherwise. My sister, the singing cashier, looks ready to cry.

'One runny egg,' I say, sliding the yellow eye and the fried bread on to a chipped plate, a little border of forget-me-nots growing in a blue snarl around its edge.

'Get that down you,' I say. 'You'll feel better.'

Burns

They will try it out for summer. Together they will confront their past, the source of all their trouble, and stamp it out. That, at least, is the theory.

On this first night they sit out front, three children, their father and Robin, his new wife. The children sit on the porch-swing, staring into the sky. It is a spooky policeman-blue. The eldest boy, whose legs are longest, pushes them off the railings with his feet, his brother and sister at either side of him. Their father sits in the rocking chair, but he does not rock. Instead, he is remembering. Smells of lint and ointment, gauze packed in aluminium foil, iced vinegar for a minor scald. His new wife stands at the railings, filing her nails with an emery board. Physically she is the exact opposite of the children's mother: a plain, flat-chested woman with yellow, waist-length hair. Everyone is listening. Tall pines are grooming the wind (Who's there? it seems to ask. Who? Who?), the chair's chains creak. Down the field something rattles, a cow scratching herself against a gate perhaps. The children keep swinging, back and forth, colliding with the darkness. When the girl closes her eyes, her father picks her up and carries her inside. His sons, not wishing to be left alone with their stepmother, soon follow.

[85]

The bedroom light comes on, shines out feebly through dirty panes. Robin hears mattresses sinking on springs, sneakers falling on wooden floors, the snap of an elastic waistband, a zipper, low voices. It is dark and starry and there are snakes in the country. The country. A gravelled road leading to a strange house, the smell of must and cattle, pools of rainwater trapped in the pot-holed yard.

Her husband comes out and walks the board floor. When he speaks, his voice is resonant and tender. She is not sorry she married him.

'Nobody's saying we can't go back, Robin. Nothing's final. You know that.'

'I know.' She reaches out, squeezes his hand.

'We have to come to terms with this thing. If it doesn't work out we can always go back to town, no damage done. You understand?'

She nods her head in the gloom.

'Christ, it's like travelling back in time. I keep expecting to hear the cutlery drawer slam. That was the kick-off: she'd whack the drawer of knives shut and you could smell trouble.' He grips the railings until his knuckles turn white. 'You see this swing? I got this put up here for the boy, so he'd be able to swing in his bare feet and cool off the scalds. Jesus.' He shakes his head, as if everything is beyond him. 'How could I have been such a fool for so long?'

'Come to bed, honey,' Robin says, taking his hand.

Their belongings, boxes and carry-alls are dumped all over the floors, but she finds her way by the glow of the children's night-light through to the back bedroom. They undress and lie down without bothering to wash. Robin pulls the blanket up around her chin. In the darkness, she can't make him out. She can't get over how dark it is out here. If somebody paid her a million dollars she wouldn't walk down that gravelled road alone. She rolls into the warmth of her husband's body, feels sleep tugging, pulling her under, and as she is giving in, letting go, she wonders if this is the side his ex-wife slept on.

In the morning, they prop the doors and windows open and a fresh wind travels through the house. Some of the window latches are stiff; there are cobwebs in every corner. The boys inspect dead moths and insects on the sills, turn them over with toothpicks, counting their legs, pulling their wings off.

'Gross!' the girl says, finding a baby cockroach under an old cornflakes box in the pantry.

A thick, white dust hangs over everything. The girl writes her name on the horizontal surfaces. (She has just recently learned to read and write.) The stuffed stag head above the fireplace looks like he's come in from the snow. Robin hates his plastic, watching eyes and there's something dreary about the kitchen, with its orange walls, the blue, wooden geese flying in a V above the sink, the wobbly kitchen table.

They breakfast on junk food, leftovers from the journey: crackers, Easi-spread, tortilla chips. Robin digs some instant coffee from a jar, boils water in a saucepan.

Much of the cutlery in the drawers is rusted. When she opens the refrigerator, she sees pickles floating in a jar of green vinegar, bulbs of dried-out garlic, shrivelled hot dogs.

'Who's for a shot of penicillin?' she says, holding up a mouldy tomato.

They explore the house after breakfast. The living area is all on the second floor; the country kitchen, a big, high-ceilinged living room, three bedrooms with baths, and a dormitory with eight single beds. (The extended family used to come up for Thanksgivings.) Off the kitchen, a junk room with a washing machine and dryer, a cradle, a wall of shelves stacked tight with paint cans, toddlers' toys, frisbees, charcoal. Everything faded from too much sun. They descend the steps from the living room down to the ground floor, which is empty. Nothing down there only a musty feeling, a concrete floor, old smells of leather, roots and mice. The middle boy stands at the top of the steps and watches them descend and return, but he does not venture down.

The yard stretches down to a black barn with stalls, hay bales, a chicken shed with toadstools inside the door. At the far end, trees are sprouting small, hard peaches. The morning sun throws this side of the house into deep and palpable shadow. Bamboo canes for supporting peas and beans still stand askew in the vegetable patch. The boys dislodge them from the earth and throw them like javelins across the tall weeds. The girl is quiet, carrying her stuffed giraffe, holding him up to peep in through the cracks in the chicken shed, the stalls in the barn, reading the brand names on empty feed bags.

When the boys ride into town with their father for supplies, Robin takes the girl down the field to pick wild flowers. The boundaries are blood-red with some shrub she cannot name. The girl points out the poison ivy, tells Robin to 'watch out', and reaches up to pluck the reddest, heaviest blooms. When she scratches the circular scar on her wrist, Robin asks if she can hold her flowers.

Quickly, the girl pulls her sleeve down and shakes her head, no.

They walk back through swishing, buttercupped grasses to the house. The girl finds old cans from plum tomatoes in the junk room, peels their faded labels off, revealing shiny silver tin underneath, and arranges the red flowers while Robin sweeps the floors.

The boys come back with brown-paper bags of groceries and McDonald's Happy Meals. Their father has brought drinking water for the fountain. When the girl climbs on to a stool, the table wobbles and her drink spills. A look of terror passes over her face. She begins to cry out of all proportion.

'Hey!' says her father. 'Hey, my baby girl, what's wrong? Here, it doesn't matter. Here, have mine.'

He sits her on his lap and gives her a sip out of his drink, dips a French fry into ketchup and tells her she is a good girl, his girl, to eat up, that soon she will be as tall as those weeds in the yard, but the girl slides down between his knees and crouches under the shelter of the table.

That night in bed, after the children have gone to sleep and doors are locked, they talk.

'Maybe I'm just opening a can of worms, coming up here,' he says. 'Taking the kids up here. Opening a big can of worms.'

'I don't think so, honey.'

'It's like the bitch is still here. I feel it. The children feel it,' he says. 'Did you see her today, just spilling her drink, how upset she was? Maybe this just isn't necessary.' He reaches out to turn the fan up a notch. 'We were in a restaurant one time and she spilled her grape juice; well, you know grape juice, the way it stains. It was a fancy place too, a white tablecloth and all. Well, she just lost her rag, reached out and whacked that little girl across the face before I could move.'

'Jesus.'

He sips water from a plastic cup. Some of the hairs on his belly have turned white.

'Maybe we should do the place up different, make it over, change things round,' Robin says. 'We could ask some of the kids' friends up. It's not like there isn't room.'

'Maybe.' He wipes his forehead. 'Maybe we should shake holy water around, get the preacher in. Maybe we should set a match to this place and high-tail it out of here. Go back home, get our heads examined.'

'Don't worry,' she says, scratching his hair. 'Everything'll be okay, you'll see.'

'I hope so,' he says, punching up the pillows. 'I certainly hope so.'

The first thing they tackle is the kitchen. They move out all the furniture, the dresser, the wobbly table, take the wooden ducks and the fire extinguisher off the walls and empty out the cabinets. They draw a design for a new kitchen on the back of an old Whitney Bank calendar. An island is what they decide on. Something they can all sit around and cook at. They let each child choose a name from *Carpenters* in the Yellow Pages and call for estimates.

When the week's over, their island is built in the centre of the kitchen. Nothing fancy, just a tall rectangular counter with cabinets underneath. The gas man has piped in a supply for a hob. Robin takes the girl down to the co-op, and they choose pretty, brick-red tiles for the counter tops, two dozen decorative tiles with beige leaves for the border. Together they mix grout in a basin and lay it all down. She lets the girl stay up late to help her while everybody else is sleeping. She buys five tall directors' chairs, the kind where you can take the canvas seats off and throw them in the washing machine, gets an electrician to install dimmer switches above the hob. The boys screw crooks into the beam overhead and hang all the cooking utensils from the ceiling.

The night it's finished their father drives down to the Winn Dixie market for root beer. Robin has a tray of lasagne in the oven and she's baking a chocolate cake for dessert. The kids kneel on the directors' chairs around the island and help out. Robin puts the eldest boy in charge of sifting the flour and cocoa while she beats the butter and sugar with a wooden spoon. The girl measures out the teaspoons of baking powder and corn starch and greases the tin with butter while her brother whisks the eggs. Robin gives everyone a turn at the mixing bowl, smiles at the girl, who is left-handed and mixes counter-clockwise. Robin checks the oven, pours the batter in the tin. The children lick the bowl clean.

'Okay,' says Robin, 'your dad'll be home soon. Let's clear up.'

Robin lights a candle and places it on the middle of the island, dims the lights. Seeing the girl's red flowers on the sill, she reaches, and it's then she notices something at her feet. At first she thinks it's a mouse. She is not afraid of mice. The girl is the first to scream. The children instinctively climb up on the island for safety and knock the lighted candle over.

And that is how their father finds them, his three children and his new wife screaming, a naked flame, a fire starting in the kitchen, and the floor moving. He douses the candle, quickly before it catches, and looks down at the floor. He has never seen anything like it. For some reason he cannot move. Instead, he remembers an old black-and-white movie with locusts descending on a field somewhere in Africa, wiping out an entire crop, a livelihood, in minutes.

Cockroaches are everywhere. Hard-bodied, shiny roaches. They are crawling around the island, scuttling up the cabinet doors, behind the taps, underneath the water fountain. They swirl in behind the red flowers that smell like cat piss on the sill. The sound they make is not unlike the sound of drizzling rain. The children are standing on the island. The eldest boy reaches for the cooking utensils on the beam, the serving spoon, the fish-slice, the ladle, and hands them to his siblings. They start killing. They stamp on them with their sneakers. The girl, reluctant at first, rolls her sleeves up to get a good whack at them. Robin runs into the junk room. Her shoes make an awful sound with every step. She brings out tennis racquets and a plastic baseball bat and she too starts killing. Her husband is mesmerised. His new wife is killing with both hands.

'Don't just stand there!' she screams. 'Help us!'

She hands him the baseball bat, opens a cabinet door under the island and a fresh invasion spills out on the floor. A darting stream is crawling up from what seems to be the heart of the house, from downstairs into the centre of the kitchen. A surge of children's voices, piercing and irreverent, thunders through the house. Everyone clambers, is covetous to kill them.

'Come on!' The father is shouting. 'Come on, you bitches!'

They cannot say how long it is before the shiny stream of roaches dwindles to a trickle and stops. The father's eyebrows are wet with sweat, the elastic in the girl's ponytail has fallen within an inch of her hair's end, the boys are breathing as they would after a football game. They do not smell their dinner burning. They are watching. They are listening. Every one, listening. They can hear their own heartbeats. When a drop of water falls, plop, into the sink, they move violently, as one.

Quare Name for a Boy

I have come home to tell you. I have walked back into
my past, my clothes too small for me, a story from a
women's magazine. Oh, I've come back before, bought
ferry crossings for engagement parties, my nephew's
christening and Christmases. That's when I met you, at
one of those dos. You chatted me up over the hors
d'oeuvres, fed me paté on melba toast as we stood
between a besequinned hostess and a man in black. I
was your Christmas fling, a thing to break the boredom
of the holidays, and you were mine. But now these suitcases have the weight of anchors on this floor I learned
to walk on. It may be I'm back for good.

My female relatives huddle round me in the bedroom,
have brought up tea, china cups and saucers excavated
from the sideboard, the clink of crockery on trays.
They're tweedy, big-boned women who like to think
they taught me right from wrong, manners and the mer-
its of hard work. Flat-bellied, temperamental women
who've given up and call it happiness. We come from
women who comfort men, men who never say no. Now
they fill their best teacups, asking about my future, asking, 'What is it you do now?' and 'What are you going to
do now?', which isn't quite the same thing.

'I'm going to write,' I say. A smutty novel, I want to add, something lecherous and bawdy, make *Fanny Hill* look like your Sunday missals.

This always brings a sneer. It's a smart answer but a queer occupation, especially at my age. They calculate my age mentally, trying to remember what happened around the time I was born, who died. They're not too sure, but I'm no spring chicken any more. I should be doing something else by now, latching myself on to some unmarried man with a steady wage and a decent car.

'You and your books,' they say, shaking their heads, squeezing the good out of the teabags.

They don't know the half of it. Don't know the disguises I've made for them, how I took twenty years off their hard-earned faces, washed the honey-blonde rinses out of their hair. How I put them in another country and changed their names. Turned them inside out like dirty old socks. The lies I've told.

I unpack my suitcases and the ritual begins. They lean in from the bed, the armchair, the windowseat, and make conversation, wondering what new clothes I have, if my shoes are patent, my dresses silk. They finger the fabric, see how deep the hems are, read the labels, ruminate:

'Nice bit a stuff in that; where'd ya come at it?'

'Be the flip, look at the mini!'

'But sure the minis are all in again, don't you know.'

'She has the legs.'

'Lovely bit of linen in that but the devil wouldn't iron it.'

'Can't beat the drip-dry, really, can ya?'

'What size is that? Would that fit me? You've put on a bit of weight if ya don't mind me saying so. But you have the height, you can carry it.'

I drape practical cotton blouses, flared elasticated skirts, across wire hangers, a black wool trouser suit, a cashmere dress. Practical shoes that belie my occupation. A pair of red high heels to confuse them. They rummage through my things, trying to find out who I am.

Eventually they retreat into the kitchen to prepare dinner. It's getting on for six: the men'll soon be home. I hear the clunk of potatoes in the sink, the clatter of saucepan lids, and soon the smell of boiled turnip drifts upstairs. I had forgotten how these back rooms bruised yellow in the evenings. I sit under the window and read with my face in the shade and my book in the sunlight and wonder if it's bad for my eyes, crossing that distance. I read *Jamaica Inn*, the first book that lured me into this deception, and think Daphne would be a good name if it's a girl.

I have arranged to meet you in Dublin. You look handsome and tall in your cowboy boots. You kiss my neck in greeting, but your lips are cold. And something I do not remember, a gold stud, peeps out of your left earlobe. You tell me the English air must suit me, that I'm blooming.

'You're looking well, whatever you're doing with

yerself over there,' you say with something that sounds like disapproval.

Irish girls should dislike England; they should stay home and raise their sons up right, stuff the chicken, snip the parsley, tolerate the blare of the Sunday game.

'I'm a hooker, did you not know?'

'Well, your tongue's not changed.' You laugh and loop your arm through mine and take me out to the coast, to Sandycove, the granite dome of Joyce's tower mushrooming into the cold afternoon sun.

'He wrote all them famous books. Imagine,' you say, 'and this is the snot-green sea.'

A ruffle of dirty sea splashes against the rocks overlooking Gentleman's Beach. I lie down and pull my coat up round me. The salt wind is sharp, would cut the arse off a girl. We stay there for a long time without saying a word, our thoughts forking out separately.

I remember the story of a young woman someplace down west. They found her in a hut her father'd built, a one-roomed place without a chimney. In a wood he'd kept her and let her die sooner than let a neighbour know. I can still see the photos: a stretcher with a body bag, another of her smiling in a school group, her head and shoulders circled.

A fishing boat passes, not so far out that we cannot hear the men's voices singing 'My! My! My! Deeelilah!' We watch them go out into deeper waters towards Howth.

You think it's funny.

'Idiots,' you say, smiling.

You have always liked other men's pleasure, taking a small share of it for yourself. I would have thought it was funny too, if I hadn't known what I know now. I used to think I could never know too much. In college, I couldn't get enough. I stacked the books up high on the bedside locker, read late into the night and traded them in for more as if learning was something you could reduce over time. But now I know too much; like an eavesdropper I feel I have overheard an irrefutable story about myself, and so I must go slowly, must keep this to myself until I'm ready. Like holding a too-full glass, not being able to move, afeared of spills.

Rain comes down along the headland; I see the gentle, grey sweep of it moving indiscriminately south. The gulls swoop down and shit on the rocks, staying ahead of the weather. I sense this is the last time we will ever be like this. Everything casual between us will end here.

'Let's shag off for a drink.'

We walk away from the sea's edge, towards the town. The pub is dark and warm, with sepia photographs of hurling teams hanging on the walls, the men in the front row genuflecting for the camera. You check the bar and I remember a gang of cronies you talked about but never introduced me to. Three middle-aged men sit at the counter with their *Evening Herald*s, circling the hot fillies, taking a chance on the dogs, talking odds. You carry two pints to a table like a man carrying the first two bucketfuls of water to put out a blaze in his own stable. Hurried, ready to go again.

We sit in red armchairs by the fire and those nights come back to me, that week between Christmas and the New Year, six days and nights spent at your mother's empty house, when I wore nothing but your clothes, your mandarin-collared shirts that came down to my knees, your thick, brown-heeled football socks. We stayed in and ate take-outs: chow mein, fresh cod and chips, the strangest Christmas food. I remember the Japanese flag hanging in the corner of the room, the centre dipped in red like a truce gone bloody. The way you took it down and snapped it out, let it fall down over my nakedness in your mother's king-sized bed. Maybe I should have known then. We used to wake in the middle of those nights and make love and coffee, and you didn't have much to say but that was fine. I sat up and listened to the cars passing through the slush, the odd bar of 'Silent Night' from the merry stragglers going home. The drizzle on the glass blistering the view of Georgian houses.

And now I wonder what it is you expect. Another six-day fling? I suspect you think I'm a woman who doesn't have the tact to let go of a small thing like a week in your mother's bed.

'Has the cat got yer tongue?' you ask.

And then all my preparations disappear. The words come out blunt and fast and irreversible. Your hand tightens round your glass. I wait for you to say something. I want you to say you love me, even though I don't love you. It might restore the balance. If I must carry the child, the least you can do is love me.

The green wood hisses in the grate, the resin oozing out from the loosening bark. Lines of connecting sparks, what my grandmother called soldiers, march across the soot, but you say nothing. Whatever you say, I'll manage. I will live out of a water-barrel and check the skies. I will learn fifteen types of wind and know the weight of tomorrow's rain by the rustle in the sycamores. Make nettle soup and dandelion bread, ask for nothing. And I won't comfort you. I will not be the woman who shelters her man same as he's a boy. That part of my people ends with me.

You watch the two fellas at the bar, young men in their early thirties with leather jackets, blue jeans, free men. You could get up and walk over there in seven or eight cowboy strides. You drink your stout until the froth settles half-way down the glass. I watch your Adam's apple moving like a stone in your throat.

'Well, the damage is done now,' you say.

I reach across the table and wipe the froth from your upper lip, but touching brings the memory of touch, and you pull away.

'What do you think of the name Daphne?'

And there it is, my decision named. No boat trip, no roll of twenty-pound notes, no bleachy white waiting room with women's dog-eared magazines.

You peer into your glass.

'It's a quare name for a boy,' you say.

You push those cold lips into a smile. Your expression

is not unlike that of the hurlers in the photograph, and I suspect pride. Because pride is something I know about. Suddenly I don't want you, won't keep you away from the boys and your smoky snooker nights. I'll drink this parting glass, but at the end of the night I'll shake your hand. I'll be damned if I'll snare you like a fox, live with you that way, look into your eyes some night years from now and discover a man whose worst regret is six furtive nights spent in his mother's bed with a woman from a Christmas do. Suddenly I wonder why I came.

'Drink up,' you say, gesturing to my glass. 'A girl in your condition needs lots of iron.'

And so I drink my pint of Irish stout, taking comfort in the fact that you've named the mineral hidden in the white stripe of its head.

Ride If You Dare

Roslin pulls into the Gator Lodge parking lot and lifts the handbrake. The signs are good: nobody around. Just a couple of cars parked out back, an old blue Buick standing next to a chipped pick-up with an ugly brown mutt panting in the cab. She hopes it isn't his. They say a man picks out a dog that's just like him on the inside, and this dog's so ugly, he knows it.

She steps out into the heat, smells something nasty in the garbage. Lunch is well over. She brushes the creases from her skirt and takes a deep breath. This better be good, she thinks, walking over the gravel in her high heels. As she strides up to the porch, a fat lizard zig-zags across the stucco. She swings the door open, feels the cold blast off the air-conditioner.

'I'll be the guy in the blue shirt,' he'd said.

'Every second guy in the world has a blue shirt: wear a hat.'

'That won't make no difference: every second guy in Mississippi wears a hat anyhow.'

'Just wear it,' she'd said.

A waitress is smoothing out a bundle of dollar bills at the bar. She stubs out her cigarette when she sees Roslin and gives her a four o'clock smile. A guy wearing a blue shirt is sitting by the windows with his back to her.

There's a cowboy hat on his table. The only customer in the place. Roslin walks right up to him.

'You Guthrie?'

'That's me. You Roslin?'

She nods.

''Fraid I got tired wearing the hat.' He gestures to his head, stupid, like she wouldn't know where a hat went. He'd planned to stand up and pull out her chair, show some manners, but Roslin's sitting down already, hooking the plastic strap of her purse over the back of her seat. She's a lot prettier than he expected. He thought she'd be a fat girl with that telephone laugh.

She thinks this mustn't be his first time. He's too cool-headed, his face is smooth as chrome, dented below the cheek-bones. Nothing to say this isn't just a casual meeting between two friends, that she isn't just some lady who's strolled in and sat down beside him 'cos there's nobody else in the joint and she needs a little company. But they aren't too concerned. Chances are, if somebody they know does walk in, they won't be honeymooners neither, lunching on this blue shift. All that thinking and talking for too long over the phone and now they're here, taking this chance, sitting opposite one another in a Mississippi watering hole with nothing to hold on to. Damn.

'I was thinking maybe you'd changed your mind,' he says, placing his palm down flat on the oilcloth. His nails are long. A band of pale skin stands out on his third finger. 'You wanna drink or something?'

'Hell, yeah. You eaten?' She pulls the red napkin out of her glass and spreads it out on her lap.

'Naw. I was holding out for you.'

He holds his menu up between them like a shield and chooses his words.

'You like seafood?'

'Sure I like seafood. What you think I am? Jewish?'

He doesn't have anything to say to that.

'Jesus, you ain't Jewish, is you?' she says.

He laughs. 'You the prettiest thing I seen in a long time,' he says, thinking it sounds like a bad line when he hears it out loud. He'd rehearsed his lines all the way over, damn near rear-ended a Corvette, and here he is saying the oldest words in the book too soon. This lady smells good. She's blonde and tanned and smart, a real windfall. She pouts her lips and looks down at the menu. There's black mascara on her eyelashes, blue shadow on the lids; he can see how dark her hair is at the roots.

They read the courses on the menu, their eyes roving over the dishes, all the hors d'oeuvres, the entrées, the dessert menu on the back, and the different beers from all over the world from the drinks page. Roslin could go for a big fat slice of that Devil's Food cake, but the hook on her brassiere is pinching her back as it is. She hasn't worn it since they had Nelson's youngster christened up in Mobile. Guthrie thinks he better order something with no garlic, no onions neither.

The waitress comes over and takes a pencil from behind her ear.

'You folks ready?'

She keeps her eyes on his cowboy hat while she takes their orders. It's a great big hat with a feather stuck in the band. Oysters Rockefeller and dirty rice with another Bud for the cowboy. Boiled crawfish for the lady, and Scotch, straight up.

'You ain't driving?' he says.

'No. I got here on a white mule.'

'The lady's got a sense of humour. I like that.'

'Glad you approve.'

He blushes and looks out the window. The restaurant stands on stilts over the water, the muddy backwash breaking against the poles that hold them up. The sun's so bright he can hardly see, as if it's having a big orgy in the sky and blinds every eye so nobody can know what's really going on up there. That's what he's thinking when the waitress brings the drinks and crackers.

They light cigarettes because there's nothing else to say. Just a few words and it's all opened up. It's as if she's slid the zip of his pants down. She can't believe she's driven all the way out here to meet up with a guy she's never laid eyes on. One little ad placed in the *Times Picayune*, a woman wanted in bold, a few phone calls, and this. The fact that they're here says everything, and now that they've seen each other, it's done.

She takes out a Marlboro. He flicks the lid off the lighter and holds out the flame. She lowers her head and exhales through her nose, looking at him. He thinks she's like one of them movie stars, like Lauren Bacall or

Madonna or somebody, with those fancy clothes and those long fingernails. She downs her Scotch before the food arrives, leaving a thick smear of lipstick on the glass. He wishes he could tell the guys down at the mill about this. Big Andy could put that in his lunch box, but Big Andy can't hold his own water after two beers. He starts on the crackers, snatches off the plastic wrappers and gulps his beer.

'When's the last time you ate?' Roslin asks.

'Yesterday.'

When the food arrives, Roslin handles her crawfish like china and sucks the heads, throws the shells on the side and drinks her second Scotch. Guthrie piles forkfuls of dirty rice on his crackers and pushes them into the corners of his mouth, washes them down with mouthfuls of beer. He squeezes lemon juice and Tabasco on the oysters, slurps them down.

'You want me to make you one?' he says.

'Uh-uh. I'll pass. You want one of these?' she says, holding a crawfish by the claw. 'They're real good. Spicy.'

'Nah, if I start eating those things, I'll never stop. Like cookies.'

'And affairs.'

He straightens up.

'Ain't true,' he says. 'I ain't never done this before.'

'First time for everything, I guess. You placed that ad outta desperation, then, huh? Of course, if that's the case, I'm responding to desperation; don't say much for me now, do it?'

'Guess we've got something in common.'

'I never said I'm desperate; I said you was.'

'You just doing a survey then, huh?'

She laughs.

The cook pushes through the swing doors from the kitchen. He's damp around the armpits. When he goes out on to the porch, a blast of hot air swings into the room. They can feel the temperature rising.

Guthrie starts talking, tells Roslin about working down at the mill, the way Lardhead got his hand caught in the saw 'cos it was where it shouldn't have been, how he collected all that insurance money, but it was his right hand and he was right-handed. Roslin tells about how she painted the whole shotgun apartment, every room eggshell-blue, couldn't get the paint out of her hair for weeks; about that time she broke down on the highway and made a fan-belt out of her pantyhose. They skirt the conversation around their home lives, each trying to peer into the other's kitchen window without making it obvious, wondering if there's a high-chair in there.

They order another one after the dishes are taken away, and one more before he pays the bill. Roslin watches him peeling the bills off the roll.

'You didn't get nothing caught in a saw, did ya?'

'No, ma'am. All my bodily parts function just fine.'

He pulls out her chair. The waitress yawns as she collects the glasses and the five-dollar tip. When they bang the screen door, they disturb the cook having his snooze on the porch before dinner. He hears them talking about whose car they'll take, but he doesn't bother opening his eyes to see which direction they drive off in.

They take Roslin's truck, drive down through rodeo territory, past Picayune, and on towards Jackson. They don't have any idea where they're going or when they'll stop. Roslin weaves in and out between the lanes, as if driving away from home will push that feeling further away too. But the further she drives, the bigger that feeling grows. Roslin's no dumb-ass. She knows she's driving 'cos she has something to drive away from.

They talk for a bit, but it turns quiet 'cos they can't think of anything more to say. He wants to put his feet up on the dashboard while she drives, but he keeps them on the floor and smokes his cigarettes, rolls the window right down, hoping the breeze will blow his nerves away. Then the silence changes the way it sometimes does, and they're happy not talking. They just watch the signs and the high corn swaying on both sides of the highway, the gleam of the white sun on the hood.

Roslin gets to thinking about her husband. She used to call him her man. 'My man,' she'd say, even when he wasn't around. All looks and cold as a can of beer right outta the ice-box, but he has brains about the little things. Can get the whiff of Scotch on her breath even when she's brushed her teeth, knows when she buys the étoufeé from the store and spices it up when she can't be bothered cooking, even though she ditches the can. The kind of man you don't touch easy. She used to think he was like Robert DeNiro or Sean Penn or somebody. Hidden and deep. She spent ten years with him, trying to get into that place where he lived, 'cos she figured if he went to all that trouble, there must be something real precious inside, like the pearl trapped inside the oyster shell. But then she just gave up and realised there was nothing in there. Nothing. Just a hard, empty shell. He'd sunk all his energy building that thing, then he got into that groove and forgot all about what it was that he started out protecting. The day she realised that she got drunk in the living room, started right after breakfast on Scotch with ice all the way up to the top, the way she liked it. As soon as he came home and saw her lounging in her underwear, panties stuck to her in the heat, sitting in his armchair, air all sluggish, room hot as hell, fans on full-blast, trying to kick that hot air's ass, he took one look and knew she'd walk. He could tell. And she knew he could. The day you find out you've just wasted ten years ain't no picnic.

'What you thinking?'

She looks at this guy. She likes the way his shirt fits him.

'How come they call you Guthrie? I never knowed anybody by that name.'

'Oh, Mama was a big Woody Guthrie fan, so she called me after him. I'm lucky I didn't grow up on a train.' She might as well know he was white trash.

'So Woody Guthrie ain't your daddy then, huh?'

'Damn close.'

'Well, Guthrie, you wanna tune a song in on that radio?'

'Yeah. What you wanna hear?'

'Anything. So long as the damn thing ain't glum.'

He tunes in the Oldies' station. Buddy Holly, Ruby Turner, the Beatles all the way over the bypass and out the other side. They drown out Aretha Franklin, bawl along with Chuck Berry singing 'You Never Can Tell', walk the line with Johnnie Cash. Neither one can carry a tune. Guthrie whistles. She never did know anybody to whistle out of tune before. She clicks her fingers in time and her bangles shake for miles. He says it's like driving with Mister Bojangles. She almost says Mrs Bojangles but shuts her mouth up just in time. She thinks about reaching over and holding his hand and shifting the gears with it the way they did in high school. They stop for gas at the other side of Jackson and hop back in right after they pay the guy and get the six-pack, because stopping might mean turning back. They drink the Budweiser and buckle up the cans, let them clunk around the floor on the bends.

The traffic slows down and they turn down the radio to see what's going on. Men in yellow jackets are directing traffic; cars are parked up on the side of the road, far as they can see. Then they see the lights of a Ferris wheel turning on a patch of yellow sunset.

'Carnival! Jesus H! Let's go on one of those things!' Guthrie yells, leaning out the passenger window. 'Get up on that damn wheel and go way the hell up.' He figures they have to stop some time and a wet county is better than the desert.

'You wanna?'

'Yeah, I wanna do that. Get on that thing and scare the shit out of myself good.' He hasn't ridden one of those things in years.

'You crazy,' she says, but she makes the U-turn and drives into the field. They park the truck and slam the doors shut, lock the keys in the ignition but don't even notice.

'It's like Jazz Fest!' Guthrie says. 'Let's get us some more beer!'

Kids are walking around holding too many things, balloons in one hand, cotton candy in the other. Soft toys under Mama's elbow 'cos Daddy can shoot straight. Guthrie thinks it'd be a good thing if somebody tied a big helium balloon on to every one of those little waistbands, sent them all shooting right up into the sky, when the clown comes over. He's wearing one of them red noses and his white, painted face is flaking off. He takes an egg from behind Roslin's ear, and a quarter from Guthrie's.

'Now, ain't that clever?' Guthrie says. 'How'd you do that?'

'Magic,' the clown says.

'Magic, my grandma. If you could make money outta nowhere, you wouldn't be hanging out here.'

But 'magic' is all the clown will say, so Roslin gives him a dollar bill and he shoves off to the next couple.

They stand under the Ferris wheel, sipping beer from plastic cups. The seats are full of people spinning slowly round. Roslin is sick to her stomach just watching them.

'So you wanna go on that wheel?' she says.

'Damn straight. I'll get us tickets.'

'I ain't going,' she says, shaking her head.

'What you mean you ain't going?'

'You want me to sing it for you? I'd swallow raw eggs sooner than get up on that thing.'

'Aw, come on. We'll get good and scared.'

'You go.'

'You's coming with me.'

'No I ain't.'

'Well, if you ain't going, I ain't going neither.'

They stroll around the field some more, Roslin's heels sinking in the grass. There are booths with candy and ice-cream, stalls jammed full of people putting their money down on their lucky numbers for the fortune wheel, throwing darts, trying to get plastic rings over junk toys. Little fake horses making it to the finish post. There's a claw machine with its limp metal claw hanging down over all the plastic junk. They eye a stuffed seal nosing up over the giraffes, put all their quarters in and keep watching that claw drop, but it just slides across those toys every time like its battery's going dead.

'Damn!'

'Not to worry. Ain't the fish we're after,' Guthrie says as he puts his last quarter in and watches the claw dip down and rise up, empty.

The waltzer, a big, orange pot with seats, scrambles the riders, their pale faces whizzing past, screaming.

'You wanna take a turn on there?' he says.

'Uh-uh. I'd just puke up my crawfish.'

One bottle-fishing stall is for the over-twenty-ones, has bottles of liquor lined up on a table fenced off with rope. The poles holding the rope up are beginning to droop. They take a turn fishing for bottles at three bucks a turn. He eyes up a bottle of bourbon, thinking it might come in handy later on, but the cap is smooth, nothing to catch on to and the ring at the end of the pole fits tight, so he'd need a real steady hand. The guy on the end with the big buckle on his pants wins every time, so the guy who runs the stall tells him to shove off, says he has enough liquor to throw a party.

They watch riders coming down the slide. A yellow, plastic shoot that dips like a waist in the middle. Must be over a hundred feet long. People are climbing up the steps on the other side and sliding right down to the bottom like crazy on a piece of sack. MONSTER SLIDE, the sign at the bottom reads, RIDE IF YOU DARE.

'Let's get on that thing!' Guthrie says.

'Uh-uh.'

'Aw, come on. Don't you wanna go on one of these things? We can't come all the way down here and just do nothing. Show some backbone!'

'No way.'

'Life needs a little risk, Roslin,' he says. 'We can go down together. I won't let nothing happen you.'

She looks up at the people sliding down. Screaming kids, couples, old guys with the waistbands high over their bellies, out for a good time.

'It's awful high.'

He coaxes her up there. He takes her hand and they drain their beers and dump the cups on the grass. The ticket guy on the ground has a bored New York accent. He takes the money and hands over the sacks. They get in line at the foot of the narrow stairs, a steel ladder with railings on one side that go way the hell up. They rise slowly, up and up like ants along the staircase. Roslin won't look down. The speakers from the field below send up the voice of Elvis Presley singing 'Are You Lonesome Tonight?', his long, soft 'o's drifting up through the dark. Guthrie looks at the people on the ground, running around like insects. And then a young woman's voice further up is saying, 'Let me by! Let me pass! 'Scuse me!' and she's wriggling down between the riders.

'She lost her nerve,' the guy behind them says when she passes. 'But she sure is cute.'

Someone on the ground lets a balloon loose, and it sails right up close to the railings. Guthrie leans over to grab it, but it's too far out.

'Don't lean out like that,' she says. 'You scare me.' The fear in her eyes is real.

'This thing's sound as a rock, see,' Guthrie says, and jumps on the step. The whole staircase wobbles like a snake's back.

'Uh-huh. I'm going back down. Right now.' She turns and looks down at the line of people jammed in tight between the railings. The incline was gradual, their progress slow, but they're right up there. She shudders and grips the railings, shaky.

Guthrie puts his arm around her. He tries to guess her age, but she's the type where you never know. Forty? Forty-five?

'Don't think about it, honey. Just keep going. You're safe with me.' He smiles. He likes this lady from the personals. He feels drunk and optimistic all of a sudden.

They can see the man at the top now, timing the shoot, pushing their backs with his strong, automatic hand, people disappearing over the edge.

Chuck Berry comes on the speakers singing 'You Never Can Tell'.

'That's our song!'

They'd sung it twice on the journey.

'Oooh baby!'

Guthrie sings, doesn't give a damn who's there listening. Roslin looks at him, thinking about what's to come, about her old man at home. A nice big shellfish, probably sniffing out the kitchen right now looking for his dinner, reading the note she left on the ice-box. Guthrie smiles as he sings, belting out the lyrics like he's singing for his supper. That would make a nice change.

The fingertips on her shoulder feel like thimbles from all the work at the mill.

Either they are gonna do this thing or they aren't, and

right now Roslin figures they are and he isn't gonna pussyfoot around like some guys. What they want is right there on the surface. She will do this. She will go with this man in the blue shirt to some cheap motel where half the letters on the sign don't light up any more and hope it's the beginning of something. Jesus. Finally, after ten years, she's getting what she wants, somebody who'll make her feel like she's alive again, like she's somebody under her clothes. She won't stay home any longer pretending, opening all those cans, hiding 'em in the trash.

She takes off Guthrie's hat, puts it on her own head and runs the leather up under her chin. Guthrie laughs and feels the breeze lift what's left of his hair. Roslin points to her head, and says, "Fraid I got tired wearing the hat.'

'You're mighty sassy all of a sudden.'

They are almost there.

The woman before them is middle aged. The hand comes out and pushes just as she is hitching up her skirt and then she slides, screaming, down the shoot, her hair flying, and it's their turn.

They put their sacks down one on top of the other. He sits down first.

'You two going together?' the hand says.

'Yeah.'

'Well, let the lady up front.'

She hooks the strap of her purse across her shoulder and gets in between his knees. His thighs clamp instantly to her sides.

'Hold on!'

She looks down. It is even steeper than she imagined. When it happens, it happens fast. The hand doesn't ask if they're ready; it just gives them a push.

Men and Women

My father takes me places. He has artificial hips, so he needs me to open gates. To reach our house you must drive up a long lane through a wood, open two sets of gates and close them behind you so the sheep won't escape to the road. I'm handy. I get out, open the gates, my father free-wheels the Volkswagen through, I close the gates behind him and hop back into the passenger seat. To save petrol he starts the car on the run, gathering speed on the slope before the road, and then we're off to wherever my father is going on that particular day.

Sometimes it's the scrapyard, where he's looking for a spare part, or, scenting a bargain in some classified ad, we wind up in a farmer's mucky field, pulling cabbage plants or picking seed potatoes in a dusty shed. Sometimes we drive to the forge, where I stare into the water-barrel, whose surface reflects patches of the milky skies that drift past, sluggish, until the blacksmith plunges the red-hot metal down and scorches away the clouds. On Saturdays my father goes to the mart and examines sheep in the pens, feeling their backbones, looking into their mouths. If he buys just a few sheep, he doesn't bother going home for the trailer but puts them in the back of the car, and it is my job to sit between the front seats to keep them there. They shit small pebbles and say baaaah, the Suffolks' tongues dark as the raw liver we cook on Mondays. I keep them back until we get to whichever house Da stops at for a feed on the way home. Usually it's Bridie Knox's, because Bridie kills her own stock and there's always meat. The handbrake doesn't work, so when Da parks in her yard I get out and put the stone behind the wheel.

I am the girl of a thousand uses.

'Be the holy, missus, what way are ya?'

'Dan!' Bridie says, like she didn't hear the splutter of the car.

Bridie lives in a smoky little house without a husband, but she has sons who drive tractors around the fields. They're small, deeply unattractive men who patch their wellingtons. Bridie wears red lipstick and face powder, but her hands are like a man's hands. I think her head is wrong for her body, the way my dolls look when I swap their heads.

'Have you aer a bit for the child, missus? She's hungry at home,' Da says, looking at me like I'm one of those African children we give up sugar for during Lent.

'Ah now,' says Bridie, smiling at his old joke. 'That girl looks fed to me. Sit down there and I'll put the kettle on.'

'To tell you the truth, missus, I wouldn't fall out with a drop of something. I'm after being in at the mart and the price of sheep is a holy scandal.'

He talks about sheep and cattle and the weather and how this little country of ours is in a woeful state while Bridie sets the table, puts out the Chef sauce and the Colman's mustard and cuts big, thick slices off a flitch of beef or boiled ham. I sit by the window and keep an eye on the sheep who stare, bewildered, from the car. Da eats everything in sight while I build a little tower of biscuits and lick the chocolate off and give the rest to the sheepdog under the table.

When we get home, I find the fire shovel and collect the sheep-droppings from the car and roll barley on the loft.

'Where did you go?' Mammy asks.

I tell her all about our travels while we carry buckets of calf-nuts and beet-pulp across the yard. Da sits in under the shorthorn cow and milks her into a bucket. My brother sits in the sitting room beside the fire and pretends he's studying. He will do the Inter-cert. next year. My brother is going to be somebody, so he doesn't open gates or clean up shite or carry buckets. All he does is read and write and draw triangles with special pencils Da buys him for mechanical drawing. He is the brains in the family. He stays in there until he is called to dinner.

'Go down and tell Seamus his dinner is on the table,' Da says.

I have to take off my wellingtons before I go down.

'Come up and get it, you lazy fucker,' I say.

'I'll tell,' he says.

'You won't,' I say, and go back up to the kitchen, where I spoon garden peas on to his plate because he won't eat turnip or cabbage like the rest of us.

Evenings, I get my school-bag and do homework on the kitchen table while Ma watches the television we hire for winter. On Tuesdays she makes a big pot of tea before eight o'clock and sits at the range and glues herself to the programme where a man teaches a woman how to drive a car. How to change gears, to let the clutch out and give her the juice. Except for a rough woman up behind the hill who drives a tractor and a Protestant woman in the town, no woman we know drives. During the break her eyes leave the screen and travel with longing to the top shelf of the dresser, where she has hidden the spare key to the Volkswagen in the old cracked teapot. I am not supposed to know this. I sigh and continue tracing the course of the River Shannon through a piece of greaseproof paper.

On Christmas Eve I put up signs. I cut up a cardboard box and in red marker I write THIS WAY SANTA and arrows, pointing the way. I am always afraid he will get lost or not bother coming because the gates are too much trouble. I staple them on to the paling at the end of the lane and on the timber gates and one inside the door leading down to the parlour where the tree is. I put a glass of stout and a piece of cake on the coffee table for him and conclude that Santa must be drunk by Christmas morning.

[122]

Daddy takes his good hat out of the press and looks at himself in the mirror. It's a fancy hat with a stiff feather stuck down in the brim. He tightens it well down on his head to hide his bald patch.

'And where are you going on Christmas Eve?' Mammy asks.

'Going off to see a man about a pup,' he says, and bangs the door.

I go to bed and have trouble sleeping. I am the only person in my class Santa Claus still visits. I know this because the master asked, 'Who does Santa Claus still come to?' and mine was the only hand raised. I'm different, but every year I feel there is a greater chance that he will not come, that I will become like the others.

I wake at dawn and Mammy is already lighting the fire, kneeling on the hearth, ripping up newspaper, smiling. There is a terrible moment when I think maybe Santa didn't come because I said 'Come and get it, you lazy fucker,' but he does come. He leaves me the Tiny Tears doll I asked for, wrapped in the same wrapping paper we have, and I think how the postal system is like magic, how I can send a letter two days before Christmas and it reaches the North Pole overnight, even though it takes a week for a letter to reach England. Santa does not come to Seamus any more. I suspect he knows what Seamus is really doing all those evenings in the sitting room, reading *Hit 'n Run* magazines and drinking the red lemonade out of the sideboard, not using his brains at all.

Nobody's up except Mammy and me. We are the early birds. We make tea, eat toast and chocolate fingers for breakfast. Then she puts on her best apron, the one with all the strawberries, and turns on the radio, chops onions and parsley while I grate a plain loaf into crumbs. We stuff the turkey and waltz around the kitchen. Seamus and Da come down and investigate the parcels under the tree. Seamus gets a dartboard for Christmas. He hangs it on the back door and himself and Da throw darts and chalk up scores while Mammy and me put on our anoraks and feed the pigs and cattle and sheep and let the hens out.

'How come they do nothing?' I ask her. I am reaching into warm straw, feeling for eggs. The hens lay less in winter.

'They're men,' she says, as if this explains everything.

Because it is Christmas morning, I say nothing. I come inside and duck when a dart flies past my head.

'Ha! Ha!' says Seamus.

'Bulls-eye,' says Da.

On New Year's Eve it snows. Snowflakes land and melt on the window ledges. It is the end of another year. I eat a bowl of sherry trifle for breakfast and fall asleep watching Lassie on TV. I play with my dolls after dinner but get fed up filling Tiny Tears with water and squeezing it out through the hole in her backside, so I take her head off, but her neck is too thick to fit into my other dolls' bodies. I start playing darts with Seamus. He chalks two marks on the lino, one for him and another, closer to the board, for me. When I get a treble nineteen, Seamus says, 'Fluke.'

'Eighty-seven,' I say, totting up my score.

'Fluke,' he says.

'You don't know what fluke is,' I say. 'Fluke and worms. Look it up in the dictionary.'

'Exactly,' he says.

I am fed up being treated like a child. I wish I was big. I wish I could sit beside the fire and be called up to dinner and draw triangles, lick the nibs of special pencils, sit behind the wheel of a car and have someone open gates that I could drive through. Vrum! Vrum! I'd give her the holly, make a bumper-sticker that would read: CAUTION, SHEEP ON BOARD.

That night we get dressed up. Mammy wears a dark-red dress, the colour of the shorthorn cow. Her skin is freckled like somebody dipped a toothbrush in paint and splattered her. She asks me to fasten the catch on her string of pearls. I used to stand on the bed doing this, but now I'm tall, the tallest girl in my class; the master measured us. Mammy is tall and thin, but the skin on her hands is hard. I wonder if someday she will look like Bridie Knox, become part man, part woman.

Da does not do himself up. I have never known him to take a bath or wash his hair; he just changes his hat and shoes. Now he clamps his good hat down on his head and puts his shoes on. They are big black shoes he bought when he sold the Suffolk ram. He has trouble with the laces, as he finds it hard to stoop. Seamus wears a green jumper with elbow-patches, black trousers with legs like tubes and cowboy boots to make him taller.

'You'll trip up in your high heels,' I say.

We get into the Volkswagen, me and Seamus in the back and Mammy and Da up front. Even though I washed the car out, I can smell sheep-shite, a faint, pungent odour that always drags us back to where we come from. I resent this deeply. Da turns on the windscreen wiper; there's only one, and it screeches as it wipes the snow away. Crows rise from the trees, releasing shrill, hungry sounds. Because there are no doors in the back, it is Mammy who gets out to open the gates. I think she is beautiful with her pearls around her throat and her red skirt flaring out when she swings round. I wish my father would get out, that the snow would be falling on him, not on my mother in her good clothes. I've seen other fathers holding their wives' coats, holding doors open, asking if they'd like anything at the shop, bringing home bars of chocolate and ripe pears even when they say no. But Da's not like that.

Spellman Hall stands in the middle of a car park, an arch of bare, multi-coloured bulbs surrounding a crooked 'Merry Christmas' sign above the door. Inside is big as a warehouse with a slippy wooden floor and benches at the walls. Strange lights make every white garment dazzle. It's amazing. I can see the newsagent's bra through her blouse, fluff like snow on the auctioneer's trousers. The accountant has a black eye and a jumper made of grey and white wool diamonds. Overhead a globe of shattered mirror shimmers and spins slowly. At the top of the ballroom a Formica-topped table is stacked with bottles of lemonade and orange, custard-cream biscuits and cheese-and-onion Tayto. The butcher's wife stands behind, handing out the straws and taking in the money. Several of the women I know from my trips around the country are there: Bridie with her haw-red lipstick; Sarah Combs, who only last week urged my father to have a glass of sherry and gave me stale cake while she took him into the sitting room to show him her new suite of furniture; Miss Emma Jenkins, who always makes a fry and drinks coffee instead of tea and never has a sweet thing in the house because of her gastric juices.

On the stage men in red blazers and candy-striped bow-ties play drums, guitars, blow horns, and The Nerves Moran is out front, singing 'My Lovely Leitrim'. Mammy and I are first out on the floor for the cuckoo waltz, and when the music stops, she dances with Seamus. My father dances with the women from the roads. I wonder how he can dance like that and not open gates. Seamus jives with teenage girls he knows from the vocational school, hand up, arse out, and the girls spinning like blazes. Old men in their thirties ask me out.

'Will ya chance a quickstep?' they say. Or: 'How's about a half-set?'

They tell me I'm light on my feet.

'Christ, you're like a feather,' they say, and put me through my paces.

In the Paul Jones the music stops and I get stuck with a farmer who smells sour like the whiskey we make sick lambs drink in springtime, but the young fella who hushes the cattle around the ring in the mart butts in and rescues me.

'Don't mind him,' he says. 'He thinks he's the bee's knees.'

He smells of ropes, new galvanise, Jeyes Fluid.

After the half-set I get thirsty and Mammy gives me a fifty-pence piece for lemonade and raffle tickets. A slow waltz begins and Da walks across to Sarah Combs, who rises from the bench and takes her jacket off. Her shoulders are bare; I can see the top of her breasts. Mammy is sitting with her handbag on her lap, watching. There is something sad about Mammy tonight; it is all around her like when a cow dies and the truck comes to take it away. Something I don't fully understand is happening, as if a black cloud has drifted in and could burst and cause havoc. I go over and offer her my lemonade, but she just takes a little, dainty sip and thanks me. I give her half my raffle tickets, but she doesn't care. My father has his arms around Sarah Combs, dancing slow like slowness is what he wants. Seamus is leaning against the far wall with his hands in his pockets, smiling down at the blonde who hogs the mirror in the Ladies.

'Cut in on Da.'

'What?' he says.

'Cut in on Da.'

'What would I do that for?' he says.

'And you're supposed to be the one with all the brains,' I say. 'Gobshite.'

I walk across the floor and tap Sarah Combs on the back. I tap a rib. She turns, her wide patent belt gleaming in the light that is spilling from the globe above our heads.

'Excuse me,' I say, like I'm going to ask her the time.

'Tee-hee,' she says, looking down at me. Her eyeballs are cracked like the teapot on our dresser.

'I want to dance with Daddy.'

At the word 'Daddy' her face changes and she loosens her grip on my father. I take over. The man on the stage is blowing his trumpet now. My father holds my hand tight, like a punishment. I can see my mother on the bench, reaching into her bag for a hanky. Then she goes to the Ladies. There's a feeling like hatred all around Da. I get the feeling he's helpless, but I don't care. For the first time in my life I have some power. I can butt in and take over, rescue and be rescued.

There's a general hullabaloo towards midnight. Everybody's out on the floor, knees buckling, handbags swinging. The Nerves Moran counts down the seconds to the New Year and then there's kissing and hugging. Strange men squeeze me, kiss me like they're thirsty and I'm water.

My parents do not kiss. In all my life, back as far as I remember, I have never seen them touch. Once I took a friend upstairs to show her the house.

'This is Mammy's room, and this is Daddy's room,' I said.

'Your parents don't sleep in the same bed?' she said in a voice of pure amazement. And that was when I suspected that our family wasn't normal.

The band picks up the pace. Oh hokey, hokey, pokey!

'Work off them turkey dinners, shake off them plum puddings!' shouts The Nerves Moran and even the ballroom show-offs give up on their figures of eight and do the twist and jive around, and I shimmy around and knock my backside against the mart fella's backside and wind up swinging with a stranger.

Everybody stands for the national anthem. Da is wiping his forehead with a handkerchief and Seamus is panting because he's not used to the exercise. The lights come up and nothing is the same. People are red-faced and sweaty; everything's back to normal. The auctioneer takes over the microphone and thanks a whole lot of different people, and then they auction off a Charolais calf and a goat and batches of tea and sugar and buns and jam, plum puddings and mince pies. There's pebbles where the goat stood and I wonder who'll clean it up. Not until the very last does the raffle take place. The auctioneer holds out the cardboard box of stubs to the blonde.

'Dig deep,' he says. 'No peeping. First prize a bottle of whiskey.'

She takes her time, lapping up the attention.

'Come on,' he says, 'good girl, it's not the sweepstakes.'

She hands him the ticket.

'It's a – What colour is that would ya say, Jimmy? It's a

salmon-coloured ticket, number seven hundred and twenty-five. Seven two five. Serial number 3x429H. I'll give ye that again.'

It's not mine, but I'm close. I don't want the whiskey anyhow; it'd be kept for the pet lambs. I'd rather the box of Afternoon Tea biscuits that's coming up next. There's a general shuffle, a search in handbags, arse pockets. The auctioneer calls out the numbers a few times and it looks like he'll have to draw again when Mammy rises from her seat. Head held high, she walks in a straight line across the floor. A space opens in the crowd; people step aside to let her pass. Her new high-heeled shoes say clippety-clippety on the slippy floor and her red skirt is flaring. I have never seen her do this. Usually she's too shy, gives me the tickets, and I run up and collect the prize.

'Do ya like a drop of the booze, do ya, missus?' The Nerves Moran asks, reading her ticket. 'Sure wouldn't it keep ya warm on a night like tonight. No woman needs a man if she has a drop of Power's. Isn't that right? Seven twenty-five, that's the one.'

My mother is standing there in her elegant clothes and it's all wrong. She doesn't belong up there.

'Let's check the serial numbers now,' he says, drawing it out. 'I'm sorry, missus, wrong serial number. The hubby may keep you warm again tonight. Back to the old reliable.'

My mother turns and walks clippety-clippety back down the slippy floor, with everybody knowing she thought she'd won when she didn't win. And suddenly she is no longer walking, but running, running down in the bright white light, past the cloakroom, towards the door, her hair flailing out like a horse's tail behind her.

Out in the car park snow has accumulated on the trampled grass, the evergreen shelter beds, but the tarmac is wet and shiny in the headlights of cars leaving. Thick, unwavering moonlight shines steadily down on the earth. Ma, Seamus and me sit into the car, shivering, waiting for Da. We can't turn on the engine to heat the car because Da has the keys. My feet are cold as stones. A cloud of greasy steam rises from the open hatch of the chip van, a fat brown sausage painted on the chrome. All around us people are leaving, waving, calling out 'Goodnight!' and 'Happy New Year!' They're collecting their chips and driving off.

The chip van has closed its hatch and the car park is empty when Da comes out. He gets into the driver's seat, the ignition catches, a splutter, and then we're off, climbing the hill outside the village, winding around the narrow roads towards home.

'That wasn't a bad band,' Da says.

Mammy says nothing.

'I said, there was a bit of life in that band.' Louder this time.

Still Mammy says nothing.

My father begins to sing 'Far Away in Australia'. He always sings when he's angry, lets on he's in a good humour when he's raging. The lights of the town are behind us now. These roads are dark. We pass houses with lighted candles in the windows, bulbs blinking on Christmas trees, sheets of newspaper held down on the windscreens of parked cars. Da stops singing before the end of the song.

'Did you see aer a nice little thing in the hall, Seamus?'

'Nothing I'd be mad about.'

'That blonde was a nice bit of stuff.'

I think about the mart, all the men at the rails bidding for heifers and ewes. I think about Sarah Combs and how she always smells of grassy perfume when we go to her house.

The chestnut tree's boughs at the end of our lane are caked with snow. Da stops the car and we roll back a bit until he puts his foot on the brake. He is waiting for Mammy to get out and open the gates.

Mammy doesn't move.

'Have you got a pain?' he says to her.

She looks straight ahead.

'Is that door stuck or what?' he says.

'Open it yourself.'

He reaches across her and opens her door, but she slams it shut.

'Get out there and open that gate!' he barks at me.

Something tells me I should not move.

'Seamus!' he shouts. 'Seamus!'

There's not a budge out of any of us.

'By Jeeesus!' he says.

I am afraid. Outside, one corner of my THIS WAY

SANTA sign has come loose; the soggy cardboard flaps in the wind. Da turns to my mother, his voice filled with venom.

'And you walking up in your finery in front of all the neighbours, thinking you won first prize in the raffle.' He laughs and opens his door. 'Running like a tinker out of the hall.'

He gets out and there's rage in his walk, as if he's walking on hot coals. He sings: 'Far Away in Australia!' He is reaching up, taking the wire off the gate, when a gust of wind blows his hat off. The gates swing open. He stoops to retrieve his hat, but the wind nudges it further from his reach. He takes another few steps and stoops again to retrieve it, but again it is blown just out of his reach. I think of Santa Claus using the same wrapping paper as us, and suddenly I understand. There is only one obvious explanation.

My father is getting smaller. It feels as if the trees are moving, the chestnut tree whose green hands shelter us in summer is backing away. Then I realise it's the car. We are rolling, sliding backwards. No handbrake and I am not out there putting the stone behind the wheel. And that is when Mammy gets behind the wheel. She slides over into my father's seat, the driver's seat, and puts her foot on the brake. We stop going backwards. She revs up the engine and puts the car in gear. The gear-box grinds – she hasn't the clutch in far enough – but then there's a splutter and we're moving. Mammy is taking us forward, past the Santa sign, past my father, who has stopped singing, through the open gates. She drives us through the snow-covered woods. I can smell the pines. When I look back, my father is standing there watching our tail-lights. The snow is falling on him, on his bare head, on the hat that he is holding in his hands.

Sisters

It is customary for the Porters to send a postcard to say when they will be arriving. Betty waits. Each time the dog barks she finds herself going to the window at the foot of the stairs, looking out through the maidenhair fern to see if the postman is cycling up the avenue. It is almost June. The chill has slackened off; plums are getting plumper on the trees. The Porters will soon come, demanding strange foods, fresh handkerchiefs, hot-water bottles, ice.

Louisa, Betty's sister, went away to England when she was young and married Stanley Porter, a salesman who fell for her, he said, because of the way her hair fell down her back. Louisa always had beautiful hair. When they were young, Betty brushed it every night, one hundred strokes, and secured the gold braid with a piece of satin ribbon.

Betty's own hair is, and always has been, an unremarkable brown. Her hands were always her best feature, white, lady-like hands that played the organ on Sundays. Now, after years of work, her hands are ruined, the skin on her palms is hard and masculine, the knuckles enlarged; her mother's wedding band cannot be removed.

Betty lives in the homestead, the big house, as it is called. It once belonged to a Protestant landlord who sold up and moved away after a childless marriage ended. The Land Commission, who bought the estate, knocked down the three-storey section of the house and sold the remaining two-storey servants' quarters and the surrounding seventy acres to Betty's father for a small sum when he married. The house looks too small for the garden and too close to the yard, but its ivy-covered walls look handsome nonetheless. The granite archway leads to a yard with stables, a barn and lofty sheds, coach houses, kennels and a spout-house. There's a fine walled orchard at the back in which the landlord grazed an Angus bull to keep the children out, seeing as he had none of his own. The place has a history, a past. People said Parnell had a tooth pulled in the parlour. The big kitchen has a barred window, an Aga and the deal table Betty scrubs on Saturdays. The white, marble fireplace in the parlour suits the mahogany furniture. A staircase curves on to a well-lighted landing with oak doors opening into three large bedrooms overlooking the yard, and a bathroom Betty had plumbed in when her father became ill.

Betty, too, had wanted to go to England, but she stayed back to keep house. Their mother died suddenly when Betty and Louisa were small. She went out to gather wood one afternoon and dropped dead coming back through the meadow. It seemed natural for Betty, being the eldest, to step into her mother's shoes and

mind her father, a humoursome man given to violent
fits of temper. She hadn't an easy life. There were cattle
to be herded and tested, pigs to fatten, turkeys to be sent
off on the train to Dublin before Christmas. They cut the
meadow in summer and harvested a field of oats in
autumn.

Her father gave instructions and did less and less,
paid a man to come in and do the hardest work. He crit-
icised the veterinary bills, insulted the priest who came
to anoint him when he was ill, belittled Betty's cooking
and claimed that nothing was as it should have been.
Nothing was the way it used to be, he meant. He hated
change. Towards the end he'd put on his black overcoat
and walk the fields, seeing how tall the grass was in the
meadow, counting the grains of corn on the stalks, not-
ing the thinness of a cow or the rust on a gate. Then he
would come inside just before dark and say, 'Not much
time left. Not much time.'

'Don't be morbid,' Betty used to answer, and continued on; but last winter her father took to his bed, and for
the three days preceding his death he lay there roaring
and kicking his feet, calling for 'Buttermilk! Buttermilk!'
When he died on a Tuesday night, by willing himself to
die, Betty was more relieved than sorry.

Betty kept track of Louisa's progress through the
years; her wedding, which she did not attend, the birth of
her children, one boy and one girl, what Louisa had
wanted. She sent a fruit cake through the post every
Christmas, home-made fudge at Easter, and remembered

the children's birthdays, put pound notes she could not spare in cards.

Betty had been too busy for marriage. She had once walked out with a young Protestant man named Cyril Dawe her father disapproved of. Nothing ever came of it. The time for marriage and children passed for Betty. She became used to attending to her father's needs in the big house, quelling his temper, making his strong tea, ironing his shirts and polishing his good shoes on a Saturday night.

After his death she managed to live by renting out the land and cautiously spending the savings her father had left in the Allied Irish Bank. She was fifty years old. The house was hers, but a clause was put in her father's will that gave Louisa right of residence for the duration of her lifetime. Her father had always favoured Louisa. She had given him the admiration he needed, whereas Betty only fed and clothed and pacified him.

When June passes without word from the Porters, Betty becomes uneasy. She pictures the lettuce and the scallions rotting in the vegetable patch, toys with the notion of renting a guest house by the sea, of going off to Ballymoney or Cahore Point; but in her heart she knows she won't. She never goes anywhere. All she ever does is cook and clean and milk the cow she keeps for the house, attends mass on Sundays. But she likes it this way, likes having the house to herself, knowing things are as she left them.

An overwhelming sense of freedom has accompanied

the days since her father's death. She pulls weeds, keeps the gardens tidy, goes out with the secateurs on Saturdays to cut flowers for the altar. She does the things she never had time to do before: she crochets, blues the lace curtains, replaces the bulb in the Sacred Heart lamp, scrapes the moss off the horse trough and paints the archway gate. She can make jam later on when the fruit ripens. She can pit the potatoes and pickle the tomatoes in the greenhouse. Nothing, really, will go to waste if the Porters do not come. She is getting used to this idea of living through the summer alone, is humming a tune softly and weighing candied peel on the scales, when the postman wheels the bicycle up to the door.

'They're coming on the ninth off the evening ferry, Miss Elizabeth,' he says. 'They're coming as far as Enniscorthy on the bus. You'll have to send a car.' He puts the card on the dresser and slides the kettle over on the hot plate to make himself some tea. 'Not a bad day.'

Betty nods. She has only four days to get the house ready. They could have given her more notice. It seems strange, their not bringing the car, Stanley's big company car that he always takes such pride in.

The next morning she throws out her father's old vests she's used as dusters, carries the empty stout bottles up the wood and dumps them under the bushes. She takes out rugs and beats them with more vigour than is necessary, raises a flurry of dust. She hides old bedspreads at the back of the wardrobe, turns the mattresses and puts the good sheets on the beds. She always keeps good bed-linen in case she'll get sick and she wouldn't want the doctor or the priest saying her sheets are patched. She takes all the cracked and chipped plates off the dresser and arranges the good willow-pattern dinner set on the shelves. She orders bags of flour and sugar and wheaten meal from the grocer, gets down on her knees and polishes the floor until it shines.

They arrive in the avenue on a hot Friday evening. Betty takes off her apron when the taxi beeps the horn and rushes out into the avenue to greet them.

'Oh Betty!' Louisa says, as if she's surprised to see her there.

She embraces Louisa, who looks as young as ever in her white summer two-piece, her hair hanging in gold waves down her back. Her bare arms are brown with the sun.

Her son, Edward, has grown tall and lanky, a hidden young man who prefers to stay indoors; he extends a cold palm, which Betty shakes. There is little feeling in his handshake. The girl, Ruth, skips down to the old tennis court without so much as a word of hello.

'Come back here and kiss your Aunt Betty!' Louisa screams.

'Where's Stanley?'

'Oh he's busy, had to work, you know,' Louisa says. 'He may follow on later.'

'Well, you're looking great, as usual.'

Louisa's prominent white teeth are too plentiful for her smile. She accepts but does not return the compliment. The taxi-man is taking suitcases off the roof-rack. There is an awful lot of luggage. They've brought a black Labrador and books and pillows and wellingtons, a flute, raincoats, a chessboard and woolly jumpers.

'We brought cheese,' Louisa says, and hands Betty a slab of pungent Cheddar.

'How thoughtful,' Betty says, and sniffs it.

Louisa stands at the front gates and gazes out towards Mount Leinster with its ever-lighted mast, and the lush deciduous forest in the valley.

'Oh, Betty,' she says, 'it's so lovely to be home.'

'Come on in.'

Betty has the table set; two kettles stand boiling on the Aga, their spouts expelling pouty little breaths of steam. A pool of evening sunlight falls through the barred window over the cold roast chickens and potato salad.

'Poor Coventry was put in a cage for the entire journey,' Louisa says, referring to the dog. He has slumped down in front of the dresser and Betty has to slide him across the lino to get the cupboard doors open.

'Any beetroot, Aunt Elizabeth?' Edward asks.

Betty has taken great care washing the lettuce but now finds herself hoping an earwig won't crawl out of the salad bowl. Her eyesight isn't what it used to be. She scalds the teapot and cuts a loaf of brown bread into thin, dainty slices.

'I need the toilet!' Ruth announces.

'Take your elbows off the table,' Louisa instructs, and removes a hair from the butter dish.

There is too much pepper in the salad dressing and the rhubarb tart could have used more sugar, but all that's left is a few potato skins, chicken bones, greasy dishes.

When evening falls, Louisa says she'd like to sleep with Betty.

'It'll be like old times,' she says. 'You can brush my hair.'

She has developed an English accent, which Betty doesn't care for. Betty does not want Louisa in her bed. She likes being sprawled out on her double mattress, waking and sleeping when she feels like it, but she can't say no. She puts Edward in her father's room and Ruth in the other and helps Louisa drag her luggage up the stairs.

Louisa pours two measures of duty-free vodka into glasses and talks about the improvements she has made to the house in England Betty has never seen. She describes the satin floor-length curtains in the living room, which cost £25 a yard, the velvet headboards, the dishwasher that sterilises the dishes and the tumble dryer that means she doesn't have to race out to the line every time a drop of rain falls.

'No wonder Stanley's working,' Betty says, and sips the vodka. She doesn't care for the taste; it reminds her of the holy water she drank as a child, thinking it would cure her stomach aches.

'Don't you miss Daddy?' Louisa says suddenly. 'He always had such a warm welcome for us.'

Betty gives her a straight look, feels the ache in her arms after the four days' work.

'Oh. I don't mean you –'

'I know what you mean,' Betty says. 'No, I don't really miss him. He was so contrary towards the end. Going out to the fields and talking about death. But then, you brought out the sweeter side of him.'

Her father used to hold Louisa in a tight embrace when she arrived home, then stood back to look at her. He used to tell Betty to keep fig rolls in the house because she had a taste for figs. Nothing was ever too good for Louisa.

Now she unpacks her clothes, holding them up for Betty to admire. There's a linen dress with pink butterflies swooping towards the tail, a glittery scarf, a burgundy lace slip, a cashmere jacket, leather peep-toe shoes. She takes the cap off a bottle of American perfume and holds it out for Betty to sniff, but she does not spray a sample on her wrist. Louisa's clothes have the luxurious feel of money. The hems are deep, the linings satin, her shoes have leather insoles. She takes a covetous pride in her belongings, but then Louisa has always been the fashionable one.

Before she went to England Louisa got a job housekeeping for a rich woman in Killiney. Once, Betty took the train to Dublin to spend a day with her. When Louisa saw her at Heuston station with her country suit and her brown handbag, she whipped the handbag from her hands, fast as greased lightning, and said,

'Where do you think you're going with that old thing?'
and pushed it down in her shopping bag.

Now she sits at the dressing table, singing an old
Latin hymn while Betty brushes her hair. Betty listens to
her girlish voice and, catching a glimpse of their reflection in the mirror, realises that nobody would ever suspect they were sisters. Louisa with her gold hair and
emerald earrings, looking so much younger than her
years: Betty with her brown hair and her man's hands
and the age showing so plainly on her face.

'Chalk and cheese' was the phrase their mother used.

Edward wants a poached egg for breakfast. He sits at
the head of the table and waits for it to be put in front of
him. Betty stands at the Aga stirring porridge while
Louisa, still in her nightdress, looks into the cupboards,
inspecting their contents, seeing what there is to eat.

'I'm starving!' Ruth says. She's plump for a girl of her
age.

None of them do anything simply or quietly; they
don't mind taking up space, asking for more of this or
that. On those rare occasions when Betty goes into anyone's house, she is thankful for what she gets and
washes the dishes afterwards; but the Porters act like
they own the place.

Louisa makes cheese on toast for Ruth but eats little
herself. She just pushes her eggs around her plate with a
fork and sips her tea.

'You're miles away,' Betty says.

'Just thinking.'

Betty does not press her: Louisa has always been secretive. When she was beaten in school, she never said one word at home. Being falsely blamed for laughing or talking out of turn, Louisa would blankly kneel down in front of the picture of Saint Anthony and confess and take undue punishment without ever a mention. Once, after the headmaster hit Betty, her nose would not stop bleeding and he sent her out to the stream to wash her face, but she ran home across the fields and told her mother, who walked her back up to the school, into the classroom, and told the headmaster that if he laid so much as another finger on her girls, he'd get a worse death than Billy the Buttermaker (who had been savagely murdered down south a few days back). Louisa had jeered her about that, but Betty was unashamed. She would rather tell the truth and face the consequences than get down on her knees before a picture of a saint and confess to things she did not do.

On Sunday morning, Louisa balances their father's old shaving mirror on the crucifix in Betty's window and plucks her eyebrows into perfect semi-circles. Betty milks the cow and digs potatoes and gets ready for mass.

A great fuss is made over Louisa in the chapel. Neighbours come up to her in the graveyard and shake her hand, and say she's looking wonderful.

'Aren't you looking great?'

'You haven't aged one bit.'

'Sure weren't you always the apple of everybody's eye?'

'Doesn't she look great, Betty?'

When they go into the grocer's for messages, Joe Costello, the bachelor who owns the quarry and rents out Betty's land, corners Louisa between the tinned goods and the cold meats counter and asks is she still fond of the cinema? He's a great big man with a pin-stripe suit and a black, pencil moustache. They used to cycle to the pictures together before Louisa went off to England. Edward is setting mousetraps in the hardware shelves and Ruth's ice-cream cone is dripping down the front of her dress, but Louisa takes no notice.

'Where's the hubby?' Joe Costello is asking Louisa.

'Oh, he had to work.'

'Ah yes, I know the feeling. The work never ends.'

When they get home, Betty ties her apron round her waist and puts the dinner on. She likes Sundays, listening to the curate read the gospel, meeting the neighbours, listening to the spit of the roast while she reads the paper, tending the garden in the afternoon and taking a walk around the wood. She always tries to keep it a day of rest, keep it holy.

'Don't you ever get lonely up here on your own?' Louisa asks.

'No.' It had never occurred to her to be lonely.

Louisa paces the kitchen floor until dinner time, then takes off down the avenue to visit the neighbours' houses. Betty stays at home and works out a menu for the week. Louisa hasn't given her a penny towards their keep, hasn't bought so much as a loaf. Betty's budget is tight enough without feeding three extra people, but she assumes it's something Louisa will put right when it comes into her mind. Louisa has always been forgetful about the essentials.

Monday is washing day. The Porters don't believe in wearing the same clothes twice, and since Ruth wets the bed, she needs clean sheets every day. Betty wonders at the child – she's almost nine years old – but says nothing to Louisa, sensing it would be a sore point. The clothes-line hanging between the lime trees is laden, but a strong wind throws the laundry into a horizontal flapping state that Betty finds pleasurable. Some of the clothes are delicate and Betty must wash them by hand. As she dips her hands down into the sinkful of soapy water, she begins to wonder when Stanley will arrive. He would take them off to the seaside and skim pebbles across the waves and keep the children occupied. Go fishing for pike in the Slaney, shoot rabbits.

Betty rises earlier to have more time to herself. The summer mornings feel healthy and cool. She sits with her head leant against the warmth of the cow's side and watches milk dancing in the bucket. She feeds the geese and pulls carrots and parsnips from the vegetable patch. Mount Leinster looks gratifyingly unchanged in the blue distance; swallows are building under the eaves of the granite stables. This is the life she wants to lead, the good life.

She is pouring warm milk through a piece of muslin when Joe Costello blocks the daylight in the doorway.

'Morning, Betty.' He tips his hat respectfully.

'Good morning, Joe!' She's surprised to see him, he so seldom drops in, except when a bullock goes missing or to pay the rent on the land.

'Sit down, won't you?'

He sits in at the table, all arms and legs. 'Nice spell of weather we're having.'

'Couldn't ask for nicer.'

She makes tea and sits talking to Joe at the table. He's a decent sort of man, Betty thinks, the way he takes his hat off and uses the spoon for the jam instead of pushing his knife down into the pot. Table manners say so much. They talk about cattle and the quarry and then Edward appears, pokes his nose into the implements on the sink.

'Isn't the milk here pasteurised, Aunt Betty?'

Betty laughs with Joe Costello over the good of it, but when Louisa comes down Joe loses all interest in Betty. Louisa isn't wearing her nightdress. Her hair is brushed and she's in her linen butterfly dress, her mouth shiny with Vaseline.

'Ah, Joe!' she says, as if she didn't know he was there.

'Morning, Louisa.' He stands up, as if she's the Queen.

Betty takes it all in, how Louisa flirts: the pout of her lips, the tilt of her hip, the way she lifts and relaxes her bare shoulder. It is a fine art. She leaves them there talking in the kitchen and strides out to the garden for parsley. Ruth is standing under the tree, eating her plums.

'Get away from those plums!'

'Okay, okay,' Ruth says. 'Don't get your knickers in a knot.'

'They're for jam.'

It is an old story. The men flocking round Louisa, sniffing her out, always asking her to dance in the old days.

Louisa and Betty had gone to house-dances together when they were young. Betty remembers a fine summer's night, sitting on a wooden bench in Davis's, just a mile up the road. She was sitting there feeling the grain of the wood under her fingers. The scent of lilacs from the ditch came through the open window. She remembers the happiness of that moment being broken when Louisa leaned over. She can still, to this day, remember her exact words:

'I'll give you a piece of advice. You should try not to smile. You look terrible when you smile.'

Betty didn't smile for years afterwards without remembering this remark. She never had Louisa's white smile. She'd suffered from bronchitis as a child and had to take cough medicine, which ruined her teeth. So many things, all coming back. Betty feels her blood racing when she has such memories. But that is all in the past. She can think for herself now. She has earned that right. Her father is dead. She can see things as they are, not through his eyes, nor Louisa's.

When she comes back into the kitchen with sprigs of parsley, Joe Costello is pouring tea into her best china cup for Louisa.

'Say when.'

'When,' Louisa says. She is sitting with her back to the harsh morning light, the sun intensifying the gold of her hair.

Betty cooks a leg of lamb the following Sunday. When a trickle of blood runs out on the serving plate while she is carving, she doesn't care. Nor does she care that the carrots are rubbery and overcooked, but nobody makes any mention of the meal, not one word. She's in no mood to cater for individual tastes. Earlier she had gone down into the parlour and caught Ruth jumping on the armchair. What's more, there are dog hairs all over the house. Everywhere she looks, dog hairs.

Edward hangs around, silently entering the rooms in which she's working and startles her. He cannot entertain himself.

'There's nothing to do,' he complains. 'We're stranded.'

'You can clean out the hen house if you like,' Betty says. 'The sprong's in the barn.'

But somehow this does not appeal to Edward. He's not a fellow who believes in earning his appetite. Ruth sings and skips around the garden. Betty feels sorry for her sometimes: Louisa pays her little or no attention and she needs some at her age. So when Betty is finished washing the blood-stained dishes, she reads her *Hansel and Gretel*.

'Why would the father desert his own children?' Ruth asks.

Betty cannot think of an answer.

Betty makes jam, takes the step-ladder outside, reaches up into the boughs and plucks every single plum off the tree. They are her plums. She washes and stones them, covers the fruit with sugar in the preserving pan and shows Ruth and Edward how to wash the jam jars. They haven't a clue about domestic work. Edward squirts a cupful of Fairy Liquid into the sink and they have to start again.

'Who does the washing up at home?' Betty asks. 'Oh, that's right: you have a dishwasher, I forgot.'

'A dishwasher? No we don't, Aunt Betty,' Ruth says.

They make the jam and Betty lines up the pots like ammunition in the pantry. She's wondering how long it will last, when Louisa walks into the kitchen after her day out visiting. Her expression is flushed and radiant like someone who's been swimming in deep salt waters.

'Any post?' she says.

'No.'

'Nothing?'

'Just an ESB bill.'

'Oh.'

July has passed without a word from Stanley.

In August the weather turns stormy. Rain keeps the Porters indoors, traps them in the rooms. Wet leaves cling to the window panes, black rainwater runs down between the drills in the vegetable patch. Louisa stays in bed reading romantic novels and eating cake, walks around in her nightdress till well past noon. She washes her hair with rainwater and makes Rice Krispie buns for the children. Edward plays the flute in the parlour. Betty has never heard anything like it; it's as if somebody has trapped a wild bird or a small reptile in a cage and its despairing little voice is crying out to be freed. Ruth cuts pictures of models and perfume out of magazines with Betty's good dressmaking scissors and pastes them in her scrapbook.

Betty becomes concerned about the garden. Strong winds have shaken the rose bushes, scattered the blooms across the gravel, and Betty, picking them up, feels sorry and strokes the dusky-pink petals, smooth as eyelids in her fingers. There are greenfly on the leaves; they are spotted and drowsy. She has been too busy with domestic chores to tend her garden.

She is standing there, thinking about her poor flowers, when Edward approaches her. Elderberry blossoms are being cast about like confetti in the wind; a light drizzle is falling from a sky of fragmented, greyish cloud.

'Aunt Betty?'

'Yes?'

'Who will own this place when you die?'

She's shocked. The words are like a hard, stinging slap.

'Why? I –' She can't think of anything to say.

Edward is standing there looking at her with his hands in the pockets of his linen trousers that are almost impossible to iron. She feels the sudden threat of tears, backs away from him.

[154]

'Go inside and help your mother!' she barks, but he does not move: he just stands there looking into her eyes. His eyes are narrow and blue. She retreats, walks through the ruined garden, down the avenue, and takes refuge in the woods where she cannot be seen. She sits on a damp, mossy stone under the swaying trees for a long time, thinking.

For the first time since her father's death she gives in to a flood of warm, salty tears. Things come back to her: she sees herself at Christmas time wringing turkeys' necks, a mound of feathers at her feet; as a child running in to warm her hands at the fire and running out again, hearing her mother say, 'She's such a hardy little girl.' Her mother going out to the meadow, then laid out so unexpectedly, rosary beads entwined between her fingers. She sees Louisa in a grey suit leaving on the boat to England, coming back with a wealthy husband, pictures of babies in christening robes; her father taking pride in his grandson. She remembers Cyril Dawe sitting under the hawthorn in autumn with his arms around her, holding her tight as if he was afraid she would get away. How he reached down and took a stone from under her, an act of tenderness. All her life she'd worked, she'd done the right things, but was it right? She sees herself stooping to pick up the pieces of a china plate her father broke in temper. Is this what she's become? A woman with broken plates? Is that all?

It seems to her now that there is nothing new under the sun. Edward thinks he'll step into her shoes, just as she stepped into her mother's. Inheritance is not renewal. More than anything, it keeps everything the same. All that is left, all that's sensible, is to clutch on to what is hers by right. Nothing shall ever stop her.

It is getting dark. How long has she been away? She walks up between the trees. She pacifies herself by concluding that it is only a matter of time before Louisa leaves. The children will have to be back to attend school in a fortnight's time. Come September, Betty will be able to get a good night's sleep, listen to the wireless, get rid of the dog hairs, cook when and what she likes, not have those awful children asking her what will happen when she dies.

When Betty arrives home, Louisa has spread a piece of blue cotton on the parlour floor, is putting an edge on her dressmaker's scissors with the file Betty keeps for sharpening the knives.

'I was thinking we could make some new curtains for the bathroom. Those ones you have are ancient,' she says. She puts the blade to the edge of the fabric and begins to cut.

'Do as you please,' Betty says, and goes upstairs to lie down.

The weather does not take up in mid-August. Huge grey clouds provide a sullen parchment overhead. Frogs crawl in under the door on rainy nights, and Betty finds it almost impossible to get the clothes dry. She hangs them on a clothes-horse round the Aga, lights the parlour fire, but a down-draught pushes black smoke into the room. She watches the bees robbing pollen from her crimson flowers outside the door, and counts the days.

She gets a lift into town with the insurance man and checks the balance in her bank account. Her money for August and September is used up. She takes money set aside for October and becomes imaginative with meals.

She is frying pancakes for tea one evening, the fat spattering lightly out on the draining board. The children are outside. The goslings have tried to follow the goose down the steps outside the front door, but their legs aren't long enough. They have fallen on their backs, their legs paddling the air. Ruth and Edward are turning them right-side-up with a long stick while the goose hisses at them and flaps her wings.

Louisa is sitting up next to the Aga with a blanket round her shoulders.

'When will Stanley be coming?' Betty asks. She takes an enamel plate from the gas oven.

'I can't say.'

'You can't say or you don't know?'

'I don't know.'

'The children will have to be back in school in two weeks' time.'

'Yes, I know.'

'Well?'

'Well what?'

'Well do you think he'll come before then?' Betty says,

and accidentally pours too much pancake batter into the pan.

'I don't know.'

She watches the heat dimpling the edges of the batter, wondering how she'll turn it. 'You've left Stanley.'

'Those pancakes smell nice.'

'You've left Stanley and you think you can stay here.'

'Would you like me to set the table?'

'Do you know that's the first time you've asked that since you arrived?' Betty has turned to face her.

'Is it? Edward! Ruth! Come on in for your tea!'

'Louisa!'

'I have a right to be here. It's in Daddy's will.'

Ruth runs in.

'Wash your hands,' Louisa says.

'I thought you said it was ready?' Ruth says, staring at the empty table.

'It will be, love. Soon.'

Louisa gets out of the kitchen that evening. She builds a small fire in the parlour, sits in the big armchair and starts reading *War and Peace*. Betty goes out to milk the cow. She feels a strange soothing mood of crystal clarity descend. It is all beginning to make sense. When she comes back inside, Louisa has taken a bath. She is sitting in front of the fireplace with her back to Betty, rubbing cold cream into her neck. Her hair is wrapped turban-like in a towel. Two glasses on the mantel are filled to the brim with vodka.

'Are the children in bed?'

'Yes,' Louisa says.

She hands a glass of vodka to Betty, as a peace-offering, Betty supposes. They sip in silence while the light drains out of the day.

'Let me do your hair,' says Betty suddenly. She goes upstairs for the comb. When she comes back, Louisa is sitting in front of the overmantel looking into the mirror.

Betty takes the comb from her apron pocket, gently removes the towel from Louisa's head and begins to disentangle the knots in her hair. It is waist-length, smelling strangely of fern and fruit.

'Nice shampoo.'

'Yes.'

Moonlight begins to shine brazenly through the French window. They can hear Edward snoring in the big room above their heads.

Betty pulls the comb's teeth through the damp, gold strands.

'It's like old times,' Louisa says. 'I wish I could go back. Do you ever wish that?'

'No. I'd just do the same things,' Betty says.

'Yes. You're the clever one.'

'Clever?'

'Poor old Betty, slaving away. You got what you wanted.'

'Didn't you? A husband, children, a nice house. Father was no picnic.'

A silence falls. The room seems unbearably quiet.

Betty has been so busy, she has forgotten to wind the grandfather clock. A slice of winterish air slides in under the door.

'There are no satin curtains,' Betty says.

'Whatever do you mean?'

'The dishwasher, the tumble dryer. You made it up. It's all made up.'

'That isn't true.'

Louisa is still admiring herself in the overmantel. She sits there like someone drugged, who cannot take her eyes off her reflection. She won't meet Betty's eyes in the mirror. She doesn't care that Betty did without, sent pound notes to her children, carried buckets through the yard, threw over a chance of marriage, spread dung and washed her father's underpants for decades. She believes she can come and live here, encroach on Betty's ground, have her running around like a slave after her and her young family till the end of her days.

Betty reaches into her apron pocket. If Louisa feels the cold, high up on her neck, she doesn't react. She does not see the gleam of metal, the blades newly sharpened by her own hand. Betty holds the scissors, makes one swift cut. It only takes a second. Betty has great strength in her hands. She is still holding the scissors when Louisa, sensing the difference, sees her hair on the carpet.

Louisa is screaming and saying things, half-truths. Something about greed and a big house all to herself and having not an ounce of sympathy. But Betty isn't listening any more.

Louisa cries. She cries all night, while she packs, and all morning as she leads the children and the dog from the house. Betty says nothing. She just stands in the doorway looking out at the fine blue morning and smiles her terrible smile.

Louisa looks nothing without her hair.

A Scent of Winter

Whenever he thought about it afterwards, Hanson never could say why he took the kids and the young nanny down to Greer's that Sunday. Greer was in a bad way, deep in something Hanson shouldn't have been next or near to. But the fact of the matter was he did go. And he did take the children.

It was a hot fall day, but the evening wind had about it the scent of winter. It blew down casually from the North and shook summer from the trees. Hanson left his wife, Lily, heavy with their third child, sleeping on the couch. He did not want to wake her, so he left a note: 'Gone to Greer's, be back soon', with kisses, xed in pencil. He stuck it to the refrigerator door with a magnet.

Hanson took it easy, drove with the windows down. A smell of burnt leaves, smoke from a fire, and something else too, like burnt flesh, wafted into the station wagon. It made Hanson uneasy; maybe it was some farmer burning a dead sheep. The boy whined and the nanny put her arm around him, read a story from a picture book as they drove. When Hanson slowed at a steel gate, the nanny took her cue, got out and opened it, and fastened it behind them. They turned down the long, dirt road, where a path of green weeds grew up between the tyre marks. They passed a brick shed with a heavy, bolted door, quarter horses grazing inside a barbed wire fence. Tall shrubs shaded the road, their limbs beating softly against the wind.

Ted Greer came down the back steps wearing a straw hat, and shook Hanson's hand. A stocky, indecent-looking man with muddy pants and a creased white shirt. He smiled half-heartedly, showing teeth too white to be real. 'Hey there,' he said to the kids, and mussed up their hair. They carried fishing poles and the ice-box down to the lake, and stood on the white sand. The lake was round and silver as a nickel. Ted Greer reached into a feed bag and sprinkled food on the water's surface, and a barrage of hungry catfish swam to the surface and gobbled up the pellets. The nanny undid the knots from the children's lines. They didn't need bait. The catfish snagged on the bare hooks and the children backed into the shore and watched them die on the sand.

'Must be up to three, maybe four pounds,' said Hanson.

Ted Greer bit his lower lip with his false teeth. 'Must be.'

The young nanny's heart wasn't in it. She was tired of coming to the country every weekend and catching fish they never ate. She was tired of working on Sundays. She told the kids to be careful of the hooks and slid most of the catch back in the water with her tennis shoe. The children too grew bored fishing. They scratched themselves and swore oh so softly.

'What's the matter with you, son?' said Hanson. 'Never seen a bug before?'

'He's tired, that's all,' said the nanny. 'He didn't take his nap.'

They put some dead fish in the ice-box and the nanny, sensing the men wanted to be alone, took the children for a walk.

'How is she holding up?' asked Hanson, when they were gone.

'The same.'

'Did you get a doctor?'

'Doctors'll do no good. Doctors'll put her in a hospital and drug her up, and then she'll start talking, and Christ knows what'll happen if she talks.'

'Have you told anybody about this . . . predicament you're in?'

'Predicament!' Greer shook his head. 'You lawyers use the nicest words. That's what I was afraid of all along.' He kicked something imaginary in the sand. 'Hell, no, Charles, I haven't told a damn soul. I'm sorry I told you, getting you mixed up in all this. I got myself in a real mess.' Greer dumped what was left of the feed in the water; feed dust floated on the ripples. They stood there watching the fish fight each other for the food. They stood there a long time watching that, until the food was devoured and the fish swam off into deeper water.

Greer's house was wooden, painted all over in the colour of raw liver. A row of pecan trees shaded the back rooms. Sunlight broke through the leaves and threw crumpled yellow shadows across the board floor. The kitchen smelled of ammonia and soup. Several half-eaten, greasy plates stood on the counter tops. Greer reached into the pantry shelf and his hand fastened around the neck of a whiskey bottle. Hanson noticed all the empties in the garbage can.

'You been taking comfort in the bottle?'

Greer held his gaze. 'You think maybe I should get a girl in?'

'Look, it really is none of my business. Just watch it doesn't make you careless, is all I'm saying.'

He went to the window. The nanny was kneeling on the yard with his children, turning over something in the dirt.

Greer wiped sweat from his forehead.

'And how about him? Is he healing?'

'Oh, he's healing. The nigger's on the mend. My wife is starving herself to death, but there's no end to his appetite. He's fatter 'n a hog.'

Hanson put his hand on Greer's shoulder and for one terrified moment thought Greer was going to cry. Instead he turned and reached into the cupboard for two glasses. They were dusty and he rinsed them under the tap.

'It's what happens after, what'll happen after, that's what's got me worried,' Greer said. 'I can't see any end to it, can't keep him locked up for ever. There's only one ending now, far as I can see.'

'You'll just have to make sure he doesn't talk.'

'You ever know a nigger could hold his water?'

Hanson couldn't answer that. There were things about Greer he never could understand; they never could see eye to eye on that one. They took the bottle into the lounge and sat down. The armrests were frayed with years of arms resting. Above the mantelpiece was a framed photograph of Ronald Reagan, smiling, on a campaign trail.

'If it's a question of money –' Hanson started.

Greer shook his head. 'Money'll only make it worse. No sir, money can't fix this one. I give him money, he'll come running back, looking for more.' Greer looked into Hanson's eyes. 'Oh shit, Charles, don't think I'm not grateful –'

'It's okay.' Hanson dismissed it with a wave of his hand. 'You're under a lot of pressure –'

'Pressure. Hell, sometimes I think I'm losing my mind.'

The children were climbing the pecan trees, shaking the nuts, pop, pop, down on to the concrete outside the window. The nanny had a rock in her hand. Hanson heard her say they had to be careful, to crack the shell open without smashing the pecan. She was always telling them to be careful.

The men drank in silence. A clock ticked on the wall, ticked slow like the battery was low. Hanson looked up at the clock. Suddenly, he stood up.

'Can I see her, Ted? I'd like to see her.'

'Won't do no good,' said Greer.

'If I can see her, then maybe I can understand.'

Greer put his head in his hands. Hanson looked into his whiskey, watched the ice melt while Greer composed himself. A little bubble burst on the surface of his drink. Several minutes passed. Greer put his hand in his pocket and took out a silver key. He drank his drink down and got up. There was blood on his throat where he'd nicked himself shaving. His hands were anything but steady. Hanson wondered if that's what a man looked like going to his execution. He supposed it was.

Greer led the way down a carpeted hall to the last door. He knocked softly, twice, then unlocked the door. Inside smelled strange and sour, not like anything human, anything living. The room was dim. On the wall above the bed hung a colour photograph of a woman with her hand cupping the muzzle of a bay Morgan horse. Beneath it lay the woman, drastically altered, her elbows sharp as hinges. The arms were doll-like, bruised. Greer's wife couldn't have weighed more than seventy pounds.

Greer sat on the bed and took one of her hands in his.

'Hey, my lady,' he whispered. He patted her head with his fingers.

Slowly, she turned her back on them and brought her knees up to her chin. Nobody said anything.

When they came out to the other room, Hanson said, 'Whatever you gave him, it wasn't enough.'

'Tell that to a court of law,' said Greer.

He sat down like he was made of lead. Hanson heard the wicker strain.

'I should have shot him, but it's too late now. I just didn't have it in me,' said Greer. 'I could have claimed self-defence. Now it's killing me. Most of the time I think I should've got the police. I really do. He'd have done time, real time, if I'd got a decent lawyer, somebody like you. But I look at her, my own wife, starving herself to death in that room, and I know I wouldn't be satisfied. Someday, maybe a couple months from now, I'd go down to the store and he'd be sitting out there, drinking lemonade on the porch, out loose, a free man again. Nobody does time any more. There's no justice. Whatever happened to justice in this country? That's what I'd like to know.'

Hanson was silent. Healthy, lilac sunlight was sliding through the trees. Hanson wanted to get out – it was a mistake to come – but he waited for Greer to make some move to allow him to take his leave. The blind flapped, was sucked in by the draught.

'Don't judge me, Charles. Don't you judge me. Can you look me in the eye and tell me you'd do any different if some Negro come and did that to your wife, if some guy broke into your house and raped Lily?'

Hanson didn't answer.

'Well?'

'No,' said Hanson, truthfully. 'I can't.'

When Hanson called the children to go home, there was no answer. He went outside and called their names and the nanny's name, but all he heard was the echo of his own voice and the wind in the trees. He looked at Greer. Greer looked up the dusty road. They ran out and got in the truck and drove and knew, when they saw them, that it was too late. The steel door on the shed was open. Greer hadn't put the padlock on.

'Jesus Christ,' said Hanson.

In the near distance, up ahead, a young black man, blinded by daylight, was running as fast as he could across the fields towards the highway. The nanny was screaming and the kids were screaming too, running and screaming. The men caught the children like wild animals just about a hundred yards from the shed and bundled them up and held them, panting, in their arms. The nanny screamed, 'I quit! I quit! You goddam sons-a-barbarian-bitches!' and ran in the direction of the Negro, leaving the men holding the children.

You Can't Be Too Careful

Jeremiah Ezekiel Devereux is my name. My old man was a Bible freak, but we won't go into that right now. People just call me J.E.; Butch did too, but I don't suppose that matters much. I was born October 9th, 1943, in Baton Rouge General, and we moved into 16 Kramen Street, Confucius, when I was five years old. I been living here ever since.

You'll just want to know the facts: what happened, what was said. If I'd only known, I would have stayed put that night. I'd have said I had a kidney stone or a toothache, or I was a woman having a baby and gone back to bed; but the fact was, I wanted to go. I wanted to get out on that water as bad as he did, and I wasn't about to let a small thing like instinct change my mind.

I knew Butch was no angel; I could tell that right off. And he didn't pretend to be no angel, neither. He told me about the time he came home and shot up the TV with the .22 just because he didn't like the news, but he said he was drunk. He said there was nothing worse than having guns in the house when you're drinking. He said he got rid of all the guns. I believed him. I figured he was just drunk, and I know strange shit happens when you've finished a bottle of bourbon. And man, he could drink. Believe me.

It was around 3 a.m. when he called. I don't rightly remember the exact time. Butch called out of the blue, said, remember me? I said sure, knew the voice right off. He asked was I game for a fishing trip, said he found my number, said he wanted to get down river and be out on the water before daybreak, was I interested? I didn't see nothing peculiar about that. I just figured he was in the mood to get out there on the river, get the city out of his blood. Hell, I get calls like that all the time. Fishermen sleep odd hours. I didn't think nothing of it. I told him where I'd be, where my boat was at, and he said he'd find his own way down the Delta where I told him. He said if I'd bring the gear, he'd take care of the rest. Butch said he was looking forward to it. He didn't sound drunk at the time. The cops asked me about credentials. They asked me what was Butch's last name. I didn't know his last name. I'm a fisherman; I don't ask you for no driving licence 'fore you get on my boat.

Well, my truck was parked out front and it so happened that Perot was sitting on his porch nosing around, minding everybody's business, like usual. Perot's my neighbour. It could start snowing in July and Perot would just take down your registration. Snoopy bastard. He used to be a cop – I mean a police officer, see – got some kind of dishonourable discharge; but he keeps an eye on everything that goes on round here. He still thinks he's on the force. He's still tight with his buddies down the station, I suppose. But he saw me. He nodded at me when I got in the truck. We didn't say nothing, but we nodded. He was wearing a ugly Hawaiian shirt with short sleeves when I saw him. Ask his wife what he was wearing that night. Anyhow, that man lives for the force. He wants his badge back real bad. If he thought he could get his nose back inside a station, he'd let niggers in his house and say they was white ponies.

It was still dark when I reached the river. Butch was where he said he'd be. He'd shaved his beard off since the last time I seen him, looked like he'd bin up all night. I showed him the boat and he said she was real nice. I told him hang a minute, I was gonna tune into the weather forecast on the truck radio; but Butch said he didn't want no radio on, said we was going fishing and we was going to forget about every damn thing in the world, and that was that. I didn't think nothing of it. I just thought he was impatient to get out there. He did have his hunting knife, but that ain't unusual for a man who's going fishing.

The first time I saw Butch he was stone drunk. I'd come down to New Orleans for Mardi Gras, shacked up with this brother-in-law, who had a top-floor apartment in the French Quarter. I just went down there for a good time, you know how it is. Carnival. Butch came into the picture on the Sunday afternoon. I remember it was Sunday because the people was coming out of the cathedral. I was walking round before the parades started, watching what was going on, stuff like that. Thinking back, I still don't know for sure what took me down the street Butch was on. I was on Bourbon Street earlier, checking out the strip-joints. Oh, don't get me wrong, I didn't go in there or nothing. They charge $6 for a beer in those places, so I'm told. Butch is good-looking, that's for sure. I'd've called him a lady's man, ain't that a laugh? He's about my height, but his hair is real black and he wears this straw hat, the kind they sell down the market, spray-painted black with a purple feather in it. He was just standing there on the street, singing. He wasn't the only one; there was a bunch of guys: a Negro with a horn, some beatnik guitar player, a washboard lady, but they had a piano out there too on wheels, and some skinny, weird-looking guy plucking a bass. Butch was up front. I don't remember the exact song but man, he sure could sing. It was one of those Cajun tunes and he was singing in French, but it had that Zydeco feel to it too. That's the drunkest I ever seen anybody. I was thinking: I hope a breeze don't come and knock that guy over till the song's done. That's how drunk he was. There was a little crowd bunching up, see, tourists. I saw a bunch of dollar bills in the sax case and Butch was wearing that black hat, and grinning. Great Jesus, that grin. And his voice was syrupy, with that rough edge good singers have. You know what I mean.

When he was done, I stuck my hand in my pocket looking for change and I realised this kid next to me – couldn't have been more than six inches away – had this big fat boa looped around his shoulders. I'm scared to death of snakes. That nasty snake was as close to me as you. God's truth. Come to think of it, that's what I remember most about that day. The way that snake coulda bit me, 'cos of Butch.

I saw him in a bar later on, bought him a drink, told him he could sing good, told him where I grew up. Turned out he knew Confucius; some uncle of his lived up here. I introduced myself proper, told him what I did, told him he'd be welcome up any time, we'd go out on a boat trip. Gave him my number on a barmat and that's how it come about he called me.

Well, to get back to the story, Butch and me loaded the gear into the boat. You had to watch where you put things 'cos it ain't a big boat and it could've toppled over, so we had to balance it right and Butch is a big man, weighs over 200lbs, so we had to get it right first off. He had the cooler with all them beers too, don't forget.

It was still dark, but the light was breaking. The shrimping boats were going out round that time. They seen us. Butch told me to put on the life jacket on account of it being so dark. Said if I fell over there'd be no telling how he'd find me. I remember thinking that was real thoughtful. I know Butch can't swim – he'd told me about how he nearly drowned out here – and that don't sound like the type of thing a man on the edge might do, but there's no knowing. So we just jimmied up the motor and went down river. It was cold round then. There was waves from all the big boats slapping against the stern. I'm lucky I don't get seasick; some people turn green.

Butch is a drinking man. Soon as we got down river he started drinking. He started cracking those cans like he just got in from the forty days 'n' nights. At first I didn't think nothing of it. I thought he was down with woman trouble. And there was women. I mean those ladies got in line for Butch after they heard him sing. Shit, I nearly got in line myself! Like I said, I thought nothing of it. I knew he did crazy things when he was drunk, so saying crazy things made sense, I guess. I mean, we've all felt like killing our old lady one time or another. We was fishing, see. Don't forget about the fishing. Butch has a good arm, a nice cast. He had pliers for the catfish. Every time he hooked a cat he'd reel it in and hold its mouth steady with the pliers and unhook him that way. Throw him back in. That's so the buggers won't sting him, see. Butch's got a good head on his shoulders, thinking up stuff like that. And he's the one who thought of the spark-plugs too, using old spark-plugs for weights. Butch has brains. You gotta take that into consideration. I pulled in a few nice bass: must've weighed six or seven pounds apiece. I hooked some kinda strange fish I never seen before too. It was over two, maybe three feet long, like an eel, but it wasn't no eel. Didn't have the colour. Butch took it off the hook and broke its spine. I heard it crunch, you know, like kindling. He was grinning. That scared me, the way he did that, like he had a taste for that kind of thing.

After a while he stopped baiting his lines, started talking about her being a two-bit whore, all that. Said it wasn't so much that she did it, but who she did it with that stung the most. At first I was wishing he'd just shut up and quit scaring the fish. Then he started calling her a bitch, said he loved the bitch, said he lit the gas hob and held her hand over the flame, and still she lied. I didn't try to change the subject; he was all fired up. Butch said he should have locked the door when he was going out. Said he should have put a barbed-wire fence around that house years ago. Said it served the bitch right. Those are his words.

I never been to his place but once. I stopped off at the Decatur Lounge where his gig was one night and we went back to his place. She was there. Caroline was her name, but he called her Lina. She was real young. She was a good fifteen years younger than Butch. And pretty too. She was making her own sausage. That lady could cook alright. She had long red hair and she didn't shave under her arms, I remember that. And she had all kinds of herbs growing in pots out on the balcony. There was this Billie Holiday poster hanging on the wall. Billie Holiday with a rose behind her ear, if I remember right. Butch didn't even introduce us. Maybe the trouble was starting right around then, I don't know. But she was a pretty lady. I introduced myself and she handed me a beer from the ice-box, gave me a big smile like him being an ass-hole was nothing unusual. Any man with eyes could see she was pretty. I never laid a hand on that little woman. I never did. I drank my beer and made small talk and ate the lady's food and that's all. I never touched her. I was brought up on my commandments good and proper. Coveting my neighbour's wife ain't one of the one's I ever broke.

It got hot out there. When it's calm, the sun reflects off the water, and throws the heat back up at you. Butch took off his hunting vest and I noticed he had blood on his shirt. I asked him if he had an accident and he said he had a nose-bleed. I hadn't anchored the boat and we was drifting out towards the Gulf. Some porpoises swam right past us. I didn't say anything because I didn't want to make him any madder than he already was. Maybe that was my mistake, because I think he forgot I was there. I think he was talking to himself half the time. And you should have heard the things he was saying.

He burnt her hand on the gas flame, I know that much. Things got out of hand. Apparently she made a stab at him with a ice-pick. He said the gun went off too soon for his liking. But he said he made the bitch bleed proper. He was shooting his mouth off. He said that whore turned her last trick. He said she'd never tell another lie to nobody. He turned real quiet when the beer dried up. I never seen Butch quiet. Maybe that's why I wasn't inclined to believe it at first. I guess you could say I was in some kind of denial, but you know how you hear these crazy things on the news: some guy blows his old lady's head off with a double-barrel shotgun, stuff like that? Well, there's always some little old lady from next door comes on, saying how the guy was always such a quiet man, how he never caused any trouble in the neighbourhood. Like I said, I never saw Butch when he wasn't shooting his mouth off, or singing, so when he went all quiet, I got jumpy. I knew then it was true. It wasn't just a big row they'd had and he wasn't just making it up, even though I knew he was a first-class liar. I knew he'd killed the little lady with the hair under her arms.

And there I was, almost out to sea, no land in sight, sitting in a boat with a murderer.

Butch didn't even pretend to be interested in fishing when the beer dried up. There wasn't a breeze out there and the bugs was eating us alive. Butch threw the empties overboard and let them drift out to sea. I was sweating and he was sweating too. I could smell him. I could smell myself. I could hear his boots creak. We didn't have any food. I should have picked up on that earlier, how he didn't bring all the stuff like he said he would, but it was dark when we went out. He went all quiet on me. I could hear his guts rumbling; that's how quiet it was. We sat there like that with the water slapping the boat for a long time. The sun came up right over our heads and sloped down the other side.

I'd say that was around two or three in the afternoon when I saw the boat, a little fishing boat like one of them ones you'd hire out for the day. They anchored further down river, these guys, but Butch had the rudder, moved off before they cast the first line, got the hell outta there. Got outta sight. There were no birds. I remember thinking that was strange. I tried to think what I had in my pockets. But all I had was a cigarette packet and my wallet. I didn't even have a pocket knife. Butch was sobering up, going back over everything he said in his mind, I guess. He was smoking them cigarettes, staring out into space. He didn't offer me one and I was too shaky to light my own. I had to think fast. I put myself in his shoes. I wondered what I'd do if I'd just done in my old lady and I was out there with a guy like me. Butch didn't know enough to trust me. He could've slit my throat and weighed me down with the outboard motor. Nobody would've known any better. But he didn't want to take a chance on being seen. He was waiting till dark – that's what I figured. Nobody would find me until morning at the very earliest. Hell, they might never find me. And you have to wait forty-eight hours or something before you can file a missing persons report, not that there was anybody to report me missing.

I started praying. I haven't prayed in years. I didn't think I'd ever see home again. My birthday's coming up soon. I went through my whole life in my head, wondering what it was I'd done to deserve this. I remember bullying this little kid in the first grade, thinking God was getting me back. A little cross-eyed kid with slanty handwriting. I used to bully him up good in the baseball park. Funny, the things you think of. But I mean, there I was, out on the Mississippi Delta, no land in sight, sitting in a boat with a murderer, some guy I knew from a bar who comes out and gets drunk and tells me he's just murdered his old lady. Then he's sobering up and realised he's told me. What was I supposed to do? Butch had the rudder. I didn't know what to do. I mean, what would you do?

I was just thinking I could go for him, try and get him overboard, when he made a move. Butch stood up and I thought that was it. You should never stand up in a boat. I thought my time had come. The boat started wobbling. Butch tugged at his belt, looking for his hunting knife, I figured, and I'm reeling in the line, watching him out of the corner of my eye. That's right, all this time I was still casting the line, acting like nothing was wrong, like all he was telling me was fishing stories; but then he stands up and opens his pants. I thought maybe he was a queer, that he was gonna rape me. But he just takes a piss over the edge. That's all. I thought about knocking him into the water, but I'd just made up my mind to do that when he sat back down again. I guess I just didn't have it in me.

My hands were shaking; I was having real trouble hooking the shrimp. The waves were rocking the boat and my stomach was acting up. I thought I might lose it. Then I remembered seeing a movie one time where this girl was taken by one of them serial killers and she keeps talking, keeps saying her name so he doesn't start forgetting she's real. She starts talking about her childhood and her family so it makes it harder to kill her. I couldn't stand it, him not talking anyhow, so I start saying he should cast his line and quit fooling around. I'm acting normal, saying anything I can think of, acting like I never heard one word he said. Talking weather and fish and Mardi Gras, Cajun gigs, anything. Talked about my time in school and how I kissed this Oklahoma girl down at the pier when I was sixteen. I was praying I wouldn't hook anything 'cos I knew I wouldn't be able to get the thing off the hook. I was that shaky. But the terrifying part was he didn't say nothing! He just sat there, watching me. Before I started talking, he was looking off into the distance, but soon as I said anything, he looked straight at me. I must have talked for hours, saying every fool thing I could think of, but I still couldn't stand up and he still didn't talk back, even though I asked him questions. Hell, I don't know if he heard one word I said. He looked right through me. I gave up talking around dusk. I'd watched another boat pass and Butch wasn't helping me out none, so I went back to thinking. I thought if I ever got home, I'd stay home more, I'd quit drinking. I'd get rid of the shotgun and never drink another drop and go back to the church.

The sun was going down. It was real pretty, ain't that strange? I was thinking it was a pretty evening to go out on. I could see Butch watching it, turning his head when the boat turned. I thought it would be real nice if he could sing. I know that must sound crazy, but that's what I wanted; that would have made it easier, if he'd sing a song. Butch has the best voice I ever heard, anyplace.

Then he up and said something. He said, 'What would you do?'

You'll have to understand, I was so goddam terrified. I thought all the talking was done.

I said, 'What would I do what?'

'What would you do if you came home and you knew she'd been humping some other guy all afternoon?'

I thought about it for a long time, thinking of the right thing to say; then I said, 'I'd blow her brains out, Butch. I wouldn't think twice.'

You have to understand, I would have said anything.

And you know his answer? He looked at me with that grin of his and said: 'I thought that's what you'd say.'

'Then I'd get in the truck and I wouldn't stop till I reached Canada.' That's what I told him. I said they'd be thinking he'd run off to Mexico and it'd be better if he went the other direction.

'You ever been to Canada?' he said. 'It's cold up there. Colder than a witch's tit in Canada.' Then he shook his head.

Can you believe that? This is a man with the blood of a dead lady on his shirt. But he was worried about the weather.

So I don't think he went to Canada. If you're looking for Butch, I'd drive south or west, but don't go north. You won't find Butch in Canada.

I thought he was a damned fool, going out on the river, after doing what he did; but now I know that was the smartest thing he could do. I didn't see no police hunting for a murderer down the Delta. They were searching the Interstate. And taking me with him wasn't such a bad idea, either. I mean, they'd be looking for a guy on his own.

There's one thing I'd like to make clear at this point, one thing you should know before I say another word. You have to understand, I'm no hero and I don't pretend to be one. You may look at what I did and think you may have done different. You mighta fought that man like a crocodile, pushed him overboard and cracked his head open with the oar. But you have to understand: I was faced with a life-and-death type situation. Like nothing else that ever happened to me. Like slow motion in the movies. Things slow down. Every little thing means something. When Butch twitched his eyelid, it meant something. I would have said anything to get out of that boat alive. I would've sworn an oath not to breathe a word to anyone, but that don't make me no criminal. I'm the victim of these circumstances.

Well, like I said, I'm no hero. It was getting dark. When Butch started up the motor and took the boat back upriver, it was late evening, nearly night. I didn't know what he was gonna do. I didn't have the first idea. I didn't know if he was gonna slit my throat or turn me loose or give himself up or what! I saw a trawler coming upriver behind us and Butch pulled into this lagoon and let it pass. That man knows the river. He let us drift into some reeds and killed the motor.

It was real calm out there. Like glass. I could see bass

in the water, and trout. I could see Butch's face too. He looked calm. He didn't look like a man who was about to kill somebody. Our eyes met in that water.

That's when he took his shirt off. That man has hair all over his stomach, black hair, like a baboon, he is. He told me to get out. We was right by the reeds and I got out. I could hardly stand up, my legs was shaking so bad. I don't mind telling you I was so scared I pissed my pants. I stepped on the marsh and my feet sank a bit. My heart was thumping like a rabbit, felt like my chest was gonna collapse or something. There was no place to go. It was just a little marshy island out there. Anyway, I didn't want to make any sudden moves, didn't want to spark off anything that might make him mad.

He hitched the rope up and cut a chunk off with his knife. He said if I co-operated, nothing bad would happen. He told me to behave. Funny, that cut me, the way he said that. 'Behave yourself.' I looked all around, but there wasn't one boat, not a dinghy. The moon was out. I tried talking again, tried talking sense into him. He told me to shut up and take my shirt off. I had real problems with the buttons, but I didn't want to take it off over my head because that way he coulda moved while my head was covered. Then he threw his shirt over and told me to put it on. He told me to button it up and lie down and put my hands behind my back. He put his gloves on and tore a piece off my shirt and gagged me with the sleeve. I don't breathe too good through my nose, what with my asthma and all. When he pushed me down in the

[185]

marsh, I couldn't get up. I couldn't see nothing. Nobody could see me neither, what with all the reeds. He was just standing there with his hunting knife out, watching me. Then he bends down over me, puts his mouth up real close to my ear. You wanna know what he said? 'Take it easy.' That's what he said, like he was walking out of the Decatur Lounge, going home to Lina after a gig. Shit! He reached into my pocket and took the keys to my truck and got back in the boat and headed upriver. It's a miracle I didn't die out there.

Butch is a smart man. He's maybe the smartest man alive. You may think he's just some two-bit, middle-aged Cajun singer, but that man has brains. He takes me out there, puts his shirt on me, with Lina's blood all over the damned thing. He takes off. Shit. I'm left with all that and a story he knows nobody'd believe. That's just brilliant, ain't it? I mean, that's like Einstein, that's so smart. He does something and knows no matter who I tell it to, they won't believe it. And he's right, ain't he? What do you do when the truth ain't something anybody'll believe? What do you do? Like I said, Butch has brains. He nails me, knowing what he did was incredible. Another man would have slit my throat and weighed me down with the outboard motor, but no, not Butch. Where is he now? that's what I'd like to know. Where the hell is he?

The $100 question everybody's asking me is why I didn't try to escape. Why I didn't swim out to the other boat, knowing Butch couldn't swim. I can answer that, but it's got more to do with me than it has to do with Butch and it goes back a ways. It's like this. I told you my full name and how I got it. I mentioned my old man. He was a minister down in Lafayette for a while. And he knew his Bible. I know my Bible 'cos of him. I don't know if you're familiar with the Old Testament, but some of the stuff in there would never get past the censorship board nowadays. Rape, murder, sodomy, all of that. It's all in there.

Well, one time I stole this magazine from a seven-eleven. Oh, it's way back. I couldn't have been more than ten years old. I never stole as much as a hairpin since then, I want you to know. But I stole this magazine and my daddy found out and he decided he was gonna punish me. My mama wasn't home that day. She was out organising some kind of barbecue for those holies; she was always out, organising other people's lives, making herself look good. But while she was doing that, Daddy put me in the doghouse and bolted it on the outside. It was dark in there. All that dog-poop and all. I heard him take off in the truck. I don't know how long he was gone. I just started getting lonely, when I heard him coming back, banging the truck door. He opened the doghouse and I was just about to come out when I saw what he had. He came back with a rattlesnake on a hoe. He threw that snake in with me and locked the door. I heard him talking outside. He said if I was going to act like the Devil I should know what it's like to live with the Devil. And he left me there. He left me there for a long time. It got pitch dark with the snake rattling its tail in there. My mama didn't come home till near eight o'clock that night, and I was in there since noon.

Well maybe now you'll understand. Like I told you, I'm scared to death of snakes. And therein lies the answer to the $100 question. See, I had a choice between Butch, between being in the boat with the Devil, and getting into that water with those water snakes. And sir, I chose the Devil. It's a terrible thing to happen to a man my age, you know. To go out on a boat like that and come back knowing you're a coward. It happened to me. It could happen to you too, you know. It just goes to show, you can't be too careful.

The Burning Palms

Every morning the boy dresses and leaves the house before his father wakes. It's an uphill walk for the first mile, until he reaches the old school. From there he can see her cottage in the valley, the thatched roof glistening in the wet sun. The wheat in the surrounding fields is past ripe. Farmers are waiting for fine weather to bring out the combines and save the harvest. It was a bad summer.

His grandmother's cottage is not like other houses. There's no pretty garden out front to turn people's heads, no flower beds to weed or lawn to mow. It looks worse now than ever it did. The narrow strip of ground is littered with builder's rubble, broken boards, lime bags, shards of broken glass. The Council wanted to knock the house back in April, but his grandmother would have none of it, told them it was her house, and she would do as she pleased. The boy was there the day the county engineer came out to persuade her.

'Look, missus,' he said, 'we'll build you a grand new house with a little bathroom and electricity. A snug house for your old age.'

'Who says I'll live to be old?' (She's almost eighty.)

'Well, with the help of God you will, and wouldn't it

be nice not to be dragging well-water for the rest of your days?'

'There's no water makes tea like well-water. Would ya not agree?'

'Ah now, missus –'

'Would ya like a cup of tea?'

'You must see reason –'

'Whose reason? There's no point in reasoning over something I don't want. Is there?'

The county engineer had no answer.

'Is there?'

So, instead of knocking the house, the Council built a tall block wall between the cottage and the road. Now nobody can see out, or in. The front rooms are dark and gloomy and the new plaster in the front half of the house isn't painted. It's the strangest-looking house in the parish.

The boy opens the gate and runs down to the back door. Her kitchen smells of burnt lard, coal smoke, lamp oil. He fills the teapot from the water bucket, gets her china cup and saucer off the dresser. His mother used saucers, but now his father makes do with mugs and doesn't bother with a tablecloth. His Sunday clothes aren't pressed, his shoes don't shine the way they did before.

He knocks on her back-bedroom door, puts her tea on the dressing table. She's wide awake. She doesn't sleep much, keeps odd hours, but always she waits for him to bring her tea before she rises. Lately there's a shake in her hands she can't control. She isn't able to carry a cup on a saucer without spilling the tea. The boy opens the window to drive out the smell of the chamber pot. The glass in these windows is blurred, the view's distorted. A photograph taken on his mother's wedding day is hanging crooked on the wall, his mother and father in dark suits smiling for the camera. His grandparents did not come to the wedding, did not approve of his mother marrying his father.

His grandmother was a gypsy woman once, but settled here when the boy's mother was born. Before that she travelled Ireland collecting scrap with her husband. The boy vaguely remembers his grandfather. A big man who lifted him up on to the bare back of a chestnut mare, and laughed when he was frightened.

'I was dreaming about cattle,' she says, and blows on her tea.

'We'll finish the job today, Gran.'

'Aye, I won't be sorry.'

They have been trying to finish the wallpapering all summer, but their hearts aren't in it. They wind up digging new potatoes in the plot behind the house, frying black pudding and playing Beggar-the-Knave, listening to the rain dripping on the rhubarb leaves. Most days she sends the boy down to the shop on the bicycle, gives him money for sweets and her tobacco. Then the van comes round on Fridays with the groceries and gas.

The boy takes the chamber pot from under the bed and empties it down the plot, rinses it out with rain water from the barrel. He looks at his reflection in the water's surface. His fringe is growing down over his eyes: he needs a haircut.

There's not much papering left in the front bedroom, three or four strips, a few awkward patches around the window. They used to call this 'Mammy's room'. This is where she slept; this was her room until she married the boy's father and moved into the big house up the road. They hung the first strip crooked but carried on, and now the palm trees in the pattern are leaning to the left. Outside, a gust blows the garden gate open and an empty lime bag cartwheels in the breeze. The boy must thin the paste, he must finish wallpapering today, because this is the end of summer. Tomorrow he must go back to school. He does not want to think about school because it reminds him of homework, and Saint Patrick's Day.

Saint Patrick's morning came white with frost. His father sent him back into the house for water to melt ice on the windscreen. His mother pinned shamrock in his collar, gave him a 10p coin for the collection box. She wore her good tweed suit, her linen blouse, and sang during mass. Afterwards his father drove them to his grandmother's but refused to come in. He was in a hurry. The races were on in Coolattin.

'Will I call for ye on the way home?'

'It'll be too late.' She knew he'd be the worse for drink. 'We'll walk.'

His mother stuffed a chicken and iced a sponge cake with green, runny icing. The boy went to the well for drinking water, balanced the milk can on the old steel push-chair his father'd made for him when he was just a child. He liked feeling useful, liked the greedy sound of the bucket glug-glugging the well-water, and then the shrill spill into the milk can, wheeling it back along the icy road.

The blustery trees made a carousel of shadow inside the kitchen. There were smells of baking and cauliflower cheese. A woman was singing in the transistor radio. His mother set the table, used the china, the bone-handled knives. After dinner she read *The Nationalist* while the boy did his homework. There was spelling and some maths. He hated maths; it didn't always make sense. How could a minus by a minus be a plus? Geography was his subject. He could name all the counties in Ireland, the mountains, the rivers, their tributaries, the main roads.

Towards dusk, his mother braided his grandmother's hair. Flames from the black range threw shadows on the lino, and his grandmother sprinkled oatmeal on the window ledges for the birds. Looking back, the boy would like to believe that nobody wanted to leave, that nobody wanted to put an end to that day. But that wasn't what happened.

'Okay, son, finish up; it's getting dark.'

'Ah, Mam!' The boy had finished his homework, was reading about the formation of cliffs in his geography book.

'I'm tired out, son.'

'I'm not finished my homework,' he lied.

He lied because he did not want to go home. His father would come home drunk after gambling the housekeeping. They would fight over money again.

'How long more?' his mother asked.

'I've geography to do still. Ages.'

'Well, I might have a lie down. But wake me when you're finished.'

She went into the front bedroom and closed the door.

The boy sat reading, drew diagrams of the sea cutting into the land and the land falling off into the ocean. He read in the withering light until the print grew indistinct and he had to hold the pages towards the window to see the words. His grandmother didn't like to light the lamp until it was necessary, for that, she said, marked the end of another day. Dusk was her time. She rolled her daily cigarette and sat smoking, staring at the west-facing window until the sun sank.

'You'll destroy your eyes, love.'

She got up and adjusted the wick on the oil lamp and struck the match, lowered the shade down over the flame, bathed the room in sudden, gauzy lamplight.

'Get the cake tin,' she said; 'we'll make a cupán tae.'

They ate slabs of sponge cake, played Forty-five, kept track of the score with matchsticks. The boy remembers red, burning coals keeping the cold at bay, the shuffling of cards, cinders collapsing in the grate, the smell of paraffin, the sound of cars passing close by on the road, people coming home from the races, the constant rush of wheels on the tarmacadam.

The boy was winning when it happened. Two tricks to win and he had the knave. His grandmother was robbing the queen. Then a crash, the sound of breaking glass and falling stone. At first they thought a tree had fallen on the roof.

'What in name of God?'

'Mammy!' the boy cried. When his grandmother opened the front-bedroom door a cloud of plaster dust fell into the passage. At first they couldn't see, but the transport lorry still had one headlight working. It had run off the road, had come right through the front wall into the bedroom. Inside the wreckage, his grandmother found his mother. She was crushed between the lorry and the wall. The boy saw blood. He didn't want to look. His mother's hand was hanging lifeless like the dummies in Duffy's drapery.

'Margaret!'

The driver's face was slumped over the wheel. More blood. Horses groaning. Strangers ran in with torches. Ages passed. A siren grew close and stopped. A uniformed man came in and pumped his mother's chest, and breathed air into her mouth with his own. When he shook his head, somebody led the boy from the room. He was taken out of the house, under the trees, and people told him everything would be alright. Later the shot of a gun as the horse was put down.

There was ice on the road that night. A skid on the bend, that's all it took. There was nothing to prevent it happening. Some people said it was a miracle it hadn't happened years ago, what with the house being so close to the road. It was an accident waiting to happen, they said.

Strange, dream-like days followed. Grown men shook the boy's hand, as if he too was a man. Women came into his mother's house and made sandwiches and filled cups with tea and did the washing up and put the dishes back where they did not belong. People stood around drinking and smoking in the parlour, dragging dirt in on their shoes, on to his mother's good sheepskin rug, saying what a fine woman she was. Was. People talking about his mother in the past tense, as if she was dead. But she *was* dead, the boy had to remind himself. His mother was dead.

The boy found his father in the forge after the burial. He was standing there in his Sunday clothes, curving a red-hot iron bar, making hinges to hang a gate. A half-empty whiskey bottle was standing on the shelf where he kept the tools.

'Well, son,' he said. 'I don't know how we'll manage now your mother's gone.'

When the boy didn't answer, his father started pumping life into the fire with the bellows.

The boy went outside and looked up at the stars. His mother had said the stars were angels looking down at them. His mother believed in God. People said his mother was in Heaven. He couldn't go back inside. The house was full and empty at the same time. There were snowdrops she'd arranged in a vase, a shirt she'd ironed and left for him on a wooden hanger, her furry slippers under the armchair.

The boy ran across the fields, left the track of his good shoes in the fresh clay. His heart was hammering, he was breathing hard, sweating, when he reached the cottage. The place was in a shambles. His grandmother was sitting in the rubble with a blanket around her shoulders, drinking brandy from a cup. Her hair was loose. She looked wild.

'If you'd gone home when you were told,' she said, 'your mother would be alive today.'

His grandmother is smoking a lot today, stops every time they hang a strip to roll a cigarette. Her hands are shakier than usual. There's a little trail of tobacco on the floor between the kitchen and his mother's bedroom. The palm trees look queer and out of place on these walls. It was painted a plain custard-yellow before.

The boy pastes the wall while his grandmother pastes the paper. Slap slap, say the brushes. The last strip won't fit into the corner. The palm trees are crooked. When the boy slides them into place at the bottom, they overlap at the top. He cannot fix it. *Wake me when you're finished.* He feels hot and cold at the same time. *If you'd gone home when you were told.* Tomorrow he must go back to school. She would have covered his books with wallpaper, inked his name on the collar of his new anorak. She would fry mashed potatoes, wash his lunch box and sign the exercise book to say he'd done his homework.

She would ask him to go out and make sure the latch was on the gate, fill his hot water bottle and say 'sleep tight' at bedtime.

The wallpapering is done. His grandmother is tidying up the last strip, cutting away the excess at the skirting board with a blade. Her hands are shaking, and the cut she makes is jagged. She sits down and rolls a cigarette. Tobacco falls into her lap. The boy strikes the match for her. It is getting on for dusk; light is draining from the day. The palm trees look like a storm has blown them sideways.

'It's crooked, Gran.'

'No matter. Who's to see?' She is staring out the window at the wall.

'We'll make a bonfire.' There's fire in her eyes.

They collect the scraps and rags and take them outside. She gets the oil can and the sprong from the shed and they collect all the rubbish, make a pile out front beside the wall. She douses broken ceiling boards with lamp oil and strikes the match. A blaze starts, smoke rises. Broken branches crackle in the heat; bark turns into white ash. This woodsmoke smells good. It stirs something ancient and necessary in the boy's heart. He won't go home. He will live here all winter, make fires and play cards and draw well-water and go to the shop. He will not leave his grandmother.

She is pulling withered boughs out of the ditch, pitching them on the flames. She can't get the fire big enough.

Smoke drifts out across the wall, rouses the drowsy

wasps in the fuchsia bushes at the far side of the road. Crows are circling in the sky. Caw. Caw. The Irish sound for where. Ca? Ca? they ask. Beyond the fire, the evening seems much darker; shadows are wrestling at their feet. His grandmother's feet are big; his mother's shoes wouldn't fit her. He watches her lighting the cement bag in the fire. Something in his blood tells him what she'll do. But he is stunned when she pitches it on the thatch.

'Granny!' He feels like laughing.

'Stay there.'

She goes inside. Windows open. She comes out carrying her good coat, her pension book, his mother's wedding photo. She ignites a ribbon of lamp oil in the cottage. It doesn't take long for the parlour curtains to catch fire. The wallpaper is burning, the palm trees are alight and the thatch is ablaze when the old woman takes the boy's arm. They start walking, turn the bend. There is only one place to go. The boy faces it. Debris from the house, little bits of lighted straw, pieces of the past, are travelling through the air. The road is dark, too dark to see ahead. When they reach the old school, they stop and look back at the house burning in the valley. The dead pines at the gable end are blazing. A combine harvester's headlights are moving through the wheat fields.

'It's a strange day for the harvest,' the boy says, to break the silence. He can feel rain in the air: drizzle will soon fall.

'Well, if they don't do it now, they'll never do it,' his grandmother says, and leans on him all the way home.

Passport Soup

Frank Corso has come to expect nothing. He comes home late to an empty house without fire. Tonight he gathers kindling, lights the furnace and warms his hands. For supper he fries bacon and green tomatoes and lays a place for one. His wife is hardly ever home. When she is home, she is sitting on the veranda, staring out with expectation at the asphalt road, waiting for the phone to ring. Tonight her station wagon's missing from the carport. She is probably driving along the highway, searching.

He takes a carton from the refrigerator and fills a cup with milk. He butters a slice of rye bread and cuts his bacon into small pieces. It's then he notices the photograph on the milk carton. It is a photograph of a young girl wearing dungarees. There is a gap at the front of her smile where she lost a tooth. *MISSING*, it reads in big, faint letters underneath. *Elizabeth Corso, aged nine. Disappeared from her home outside Eugene, Oregon, on September 9th. Last seen wearing a red sweatshirt and blue jeans. If you have seen this person, please call . . .* and a phone number for the police station that Frank Corso has long committed to memory.

He remembers the night Elizabeth lost that tooth. He told her to put it under her pillow, said the tooth fairy would take it and leave a gift. He'd put a dollar bill under there after she fell asleep, but he forgot to take the tooth.

'Daddy! Daddy!' she'd said the next morning. 'The tooth fairy came!'

Frank Corso has lost his appetite. He pushes his plate aside and gets up and puts the milk carton with his daughter's photograph back in the refrigerator and goes to bed. The sheets are cold. He hears a wedge of snow fall from the eaves of the roof on to the drift beneath the window. Snow falling, compounding cold. Daylight bleaches the bedroom walls before he finally sleeps.

That was Monday.

On Tuesday, when he gets home, his wife's station wagon is parked in the drive. She is in the girl's room. He can hear her in there. She has wound up the music in the girl's jewellery box. He knows she is sitting in there on the girl's bed, watching the little plastic ballerina turning on its spring, tormenting herself. He pushes the door ajar and looks in. His wife stares right through him, past him, as if there is a picture behind him he is preventing her from seeing. He has become the invisible husband.

'Hey,' he says.

He approaches, sits on the bed and puts his arm around her. She flings it off and picks up the jewellery box and walks out of the room. When Frank comes out to the den, he can see her sitting on the veranda, can hear the music, slowing as the spring loosens. Tonight he does not bother with supper. He takes a bottle of

Scotch from the drinks cabinet into the bedroom with the newspaper. He reads every word, from the headlines through the sports to the obituaries, and then he goes into the en suite bathroom and sits on the toilet. When he looks up, hanging there on the wall is an enlarged photograph of his daughter that was not there before. It is a picture taken of her as flower girl at his sister-in-law's wedding. She is wearing a white satin dress that comes down to her toes, satin-covered toes peeping out from underneath her dress. In her hands she holds a bouquet of white roses wreathed in Baby's Breath. Frank Corso sits there on the toilet and puts his face in his hands and weeps.

On Wednesday when he comes home there's no sign of her car, but the furnace is lighting and there's a note that reads: 'Gone to Maw's. Be back soon.' She has not left a note like that since before Elizabeth went missing. He takes heart in this note and takes a hot bath and puts on his dressing gown. He opens the door of the girl's room. It is exactly as she left it. He looks into her closet, slides the wooden hangers to the left, then to the right. He remembers her wearing these clothes; at least he thinks he remembers. He sniffs the underarm of a yellow sweater: nothing. He takes a colouring book from a shelf and turns the pages; it is an old book from the time before she could keep the crayon inside the lines. Frank lies down on the bed and lifts the receiver of the Mickey Mouse telephone, wonders who he can call. There is nobody. People lost contact with him; nobody knew what to say. He puts the receiver down and listens to the icy wind hustling the trees outside the window. He thinks of Elsie being out in that. He hopes, if she is alive, that she is not out in that. He would rather his little girl was dead than be out in a night like tonight.

'God forgive me,' he says.

He is standing in the cornfield where he lost her, looking for her, calling her name: Elsie! Elseeeeee! She is running, running down from the drown-deep river water's edge, towards him. He can hear her breathing, the panting of a young girl. Then another voice comes from another direction, also calling her name. She turns back, away from her father, and follows the other voice. The man who owns this voice steps into view. A black stranger, who grips her hand. Her father shouts and tells her to stop, but she keeps walking away from him, away. He can see her footprints on the dry earth (it was a summer of drought warnings when she disappeared), and he hears his own voice becoming harsh, harsher. But she keeps walking. He can feel all the cells in his body bumping together, telling his brain to move, move, but he cannot. He watches her, listens to her feet and the stranger voicing promises; and then it all fades, becomes part of the silence beyond the cornfield and the river.

Frank Corso wakes with a start in the dark of his daughter's bedroom to the ringing of the telephone. He picks up the receiver, but no one speaks. It is his wife. He knows it is his wife. He can hear her, breathing, can feel her hatred travelling through the line, into the room.

'Bad dreams?' she says and hangs up. He hears her hanging up in the other room, on the other line. He gets up and goes back into what used to be their bedroom so she can lie down in what has become hers.

Frank Corso lost his own child, in his own field at the back of his own house. Those are the facts. At one point in that late evening, she was there, and then she wasn't. It was that simple, and that hard. The police came, detectives, who asked questions: Did you have an argument? Could you tell us once again, Mister Corso, exactly what happened? Take your time. These things happen. Their little black notebooks and cigarettes, suspicion. Frank giving the same unsatisfactory answers. Then the search party, neighbours walking every inch of those fields, through the rows of corn, the meadow and the grassland where the cattle grazed. It grew dark. Rows of torchlight crossed the land, shone into ditches, hedges, into the limbs of trees. But nobody shouted or ran or cried 'We found her'. Not even the men in scuba gear who immersed themselves in water and dragged the river.

When Frank Corso pulls his sheet back, there are photographs – twelve, fifteen, twenty-two photographs. Elsie sitting on his knee, Elsie at her grandmother's, Elsie swinging in a rubber tyre, Elsie with her mother's arms around her, sitting backwards on her pony, in Disneyland, blowing out birthday candles. He gathers the photographs carefully and puts them in the sock drawer and lies down.

On Thursday Frank does not come home. He leaves the office, gets a Chinese-to-go and books into a motel room on Airline Highway. He props himself up with pillows and eats with a plastic fork and watches TV. He flicks through the channels: a talk show with some guy who was dead for a while on the operating table, a documentary about the First World War, some woman talking about how to train your dogs to sit and fetch and heel. He settles for the war, watches till it's over and then he thinks about leaving his wife. A big part of him wants to leave. The house feels like a morgue. All that blame and guilt and silence. Except for those two words – 'bad dreams' – last night, his wife has not addressed him since September. But there is a chance, a small, irretrievable chance that Elizabeth will come home and if she does, Frank will be there. She could be there now. She could have walked into the cold house with snow melting in her hair, asking where her daddy is. He dials the number; his wife picks up the phone.

'Hello.'

'Hello,' he says. 'Just called to say I'm staying out tonight. I was just wondering, you know, I was just wondering –'

The line goes dead.

On Friday not only is the furnace hot when Frank comes home, but there's a big pot of soup simmering on the hot-plate, warm bread in a basket on the table. He takes his coat off and shakes the snow off his pants, wipes his shoes on the mat. His wife is setting the table. Three forks, three knives, three soup spoons, cut-glass tumblers. Frank sits down and looks at her. She is all dressed up, wearing a blue evening dress, down to her toes. He's seen it before, but he can't say where. A string of glass beads hangs around her neck and dips down into the valley between her breasts. The ordeal has dimmed the lustre in her hair and she's thinner now, but she's still a handsome woman.

'What's going on?'

'I made supper,' she says. 'How was your day?'

He had almost forgotten the sound of her old voice.

'Are you expecting company?'

'How about a drink?' she says. 'I feel like a drink. How about you?'

'Sure,' he says. 'I'll –'

'No!' she says. 'I'll fix it. Why don't you change?'

He goes into the bedroom and loosens the knot in his tie, his shoe-laces. He changes into jogging pants, a turtle-neck sweater, finds his slippers. He pulls back the duvet, but there are no photographs between the sheets. When he goes back out in the kitchen, his wife is taking warm soup bowls from the oven with a cloth. She hands him a tumbler of Wild Turkey with a napkin around the glass and turns off the overhead light. She puts a stick of butter out on a dish and takes a ladle from the drawer. She stands before him and takes the lid off. A thick, curling steam rises between them. She smiles. When she leans over to ladle out the soup, he looks down the front of her dress. Her breasts are straining against the lace. He takes a sip of whiskey. He feels like a husband again. Maybe everything will be alright. Maybe they can overcome this. Maybe they can have another child.

'This smells good,' he says, and reaches for his soup spoon once she's seated. Then he looks into his bowl. He puts his spoon down. He starts counting, counts to nine. Floating on the surface of his soup are nine passport-sized photographs of his missing daughter. Nine greasy, discoloured photographs. He pushes the bowl away and puts his head down on his arms.

'Speciality of the house: passport soup,' his wife says.

'Stop it!'

'What's the matter, Frank? Don't you like it? You never did appreciate my cooking.'

Not until Frank throws the bowl of soup against the wall does her voice change, does she really start talking.

'You bastard. Telling Elsie about fairies, making her believe in all that crap. You lost her, Frank, you lost her! You lost our child. You useless, son of a bitch!'

She walks across the floor and slaps him, hard, with the back of her hand. Then she does it again. Frank gets down on his knees. He is kneeling before her. He holds on to the hem of her dress. Her dress is blue. He pinches the fabric between his fingers. He begs her forgiveness. She does not forgive him. She may never forgive him. She backs away. He hears blame, razor-sharp words flying like knives across the room, across his head. Words that cut him. She is tearing him asunder, putting the knife in; she is twisting the knife. Twisting. But Frank Corso feels better. It is a start. It is better than nothing.